I0703420

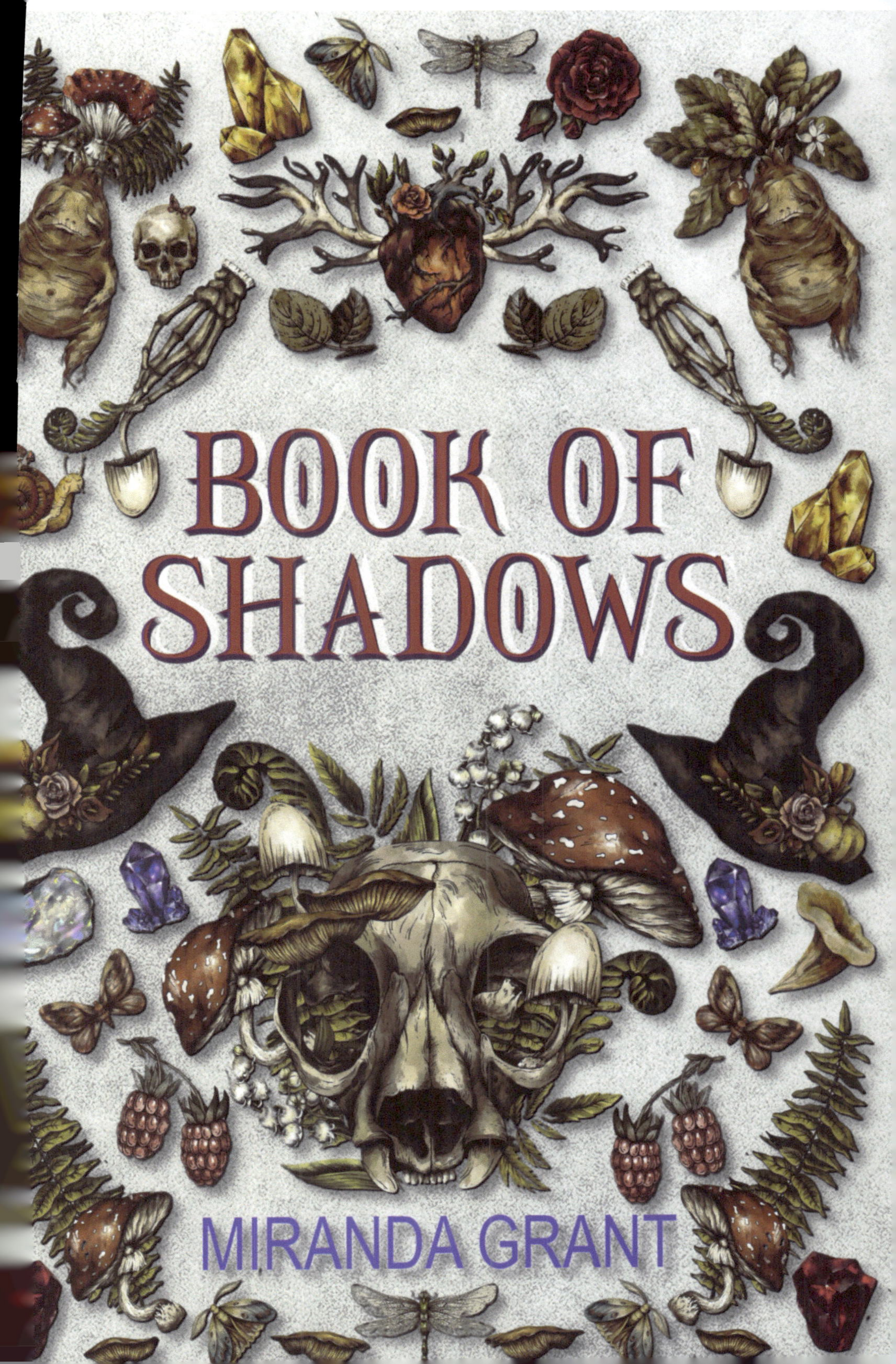
BOOK OF SHADOWS
MIRANDA GRANT

Book of Shadows

Edited and published by Writing Evolution.
   Cover design by Writing Evolution.
   Realistic coloured character artwork by Etheric Designs.
   Other character artwork drafted by Setra Nosola, traced and coloured by Writing
      Evolution.
   Black and white rough artwork by Setra Nosola.
   Mattos potions art by Writing Evolution.
      Clean-line black and white artwork by Etheric Designs.
         Magic artwork by Writing Evolution.
            Maps by Writing Evolution using Inkarnate (doesn't use AI).

Table of Contents

Dedicated To;

My onions

IYKYK

PS: This book contains SPOILERS.
Don't read Sau's page until after you've read *Jagged Souls*.
Do not read about the Shadow Girls until after you've read *Cursed to be Mine*.

THE SHADOW
DOMAIN

The Shadow Domain is one of the largest gangs in the USA. Its territory covers most of Florida and spreads up half of the eastern coast. It controls the only portal in America, which is hidden in one of their warehouses in St. Augustine, Florida, and leads to the plane known as Blódyrió, which is where the Shadow Domain migrated from two thousand years ago. They mostly deal in drugs and extortion, but they also run various legit businesses, such as marinas, butchers, landscapes, and hotels. From the latter, they collect DNA from their guests to use at crime scenes and in Khalid's soul dolls.

Unlike in most gangs, the Shadow Domain's position of Boss is inherited by the firstborn rather than claimed by a rising gang member. This is because the shadow magic only passes down through their bloodline due to the deal they made with a djinni long ago. This gives them the ability to shift into false shadows (these cannot move vertically up surfaces), travel the world of the Plane of Monsters, and open a portal to said plane. Stronger Shadows can hold these portals open well enough to allow monsters to eat anything their shadows touch, and in extremely rare cases, a Shadow can open this door even further so the monsters can come out.

However, female Bosses are seen as bad luck. Having two in a row is seen as a curse, so they are often killed in order for a son to 'become firstborn' and take the throne. If a woman does inherit and her firstborn is also a girl, then her daughter will be killed by the gang and she herself will be bred by all members until a son is born. Then whoever fathered him will rule until he is twenty-two. Ruling in the steed of their child is the only way for an outsider to be Boss.

Due to forgotten history, the current generation of women think this is a barbaric practice that needs to be abolished. But in fact, it is due to the deal they made with the djinni long ago. One day, he will come to collect what he is owed.

A woman's only purpose is to breed.

Up until 1995, the women in the Shadow Family were bred as soon as they had their first period (this was legal in Floridian law, which allowed anyone pregnant to be married off, regardless of age; once married, any statuary rape charges could not be filed). The only education these girls received was on how to serve and please men. They normally didn't meet their husbands until their wedding day as a bride's virginity could not be called into question.

However, today, due to Sau Shadow, women cannot become breedmares (not called broodmares because "they will treat us with more respect than a fucking horse" until they are eighteen. Women still serve men as second-class citizens, but they cannot be beaten anymore either, and they must be treated with respect. They still aren't allowed in any position of power though, and they are unable to fight on the front lines (though they can now be trained in combative magic), and their main purpose is still as a breedmare too, but Sau Shadow isn't done bringing change to the Shadow Domain.

Which is why she chose Micha Black to be Varius' bride.

Initiation Ritual

BOSS	INITIATE

"Show me your power."

[Reveal innate power in right hand, ball of red energy in the left]

"Will you use your magic to protect the interests of the Shadow Domain?"

"I swear it."

[Snuff out your magic]

"Show me your weapon."

[Hold up your weapon of choice]

"Will you use your weapon to protect the interests of the Shadow Domain?"

"I swear it."

[Put weapon away]

"Will you respect your brothers?"

"I swear it."

"Then hold out your arm and repeat after me."

"If I betray my vows to this family."

[First S of Shadow Domain symbol carved into initiate's dominate palm while initiate speaks]

"If I betray the Boss before me."

[Second S carved]

"If I betray my brothers and uncles."

[Third S carved]

"Then I will die under the reaper's blade."

[Boss adds his blood to initiate's]

"You now live for the Family. Until death."

"I now live for the Family. Until death."

Shadow Domain Symbol

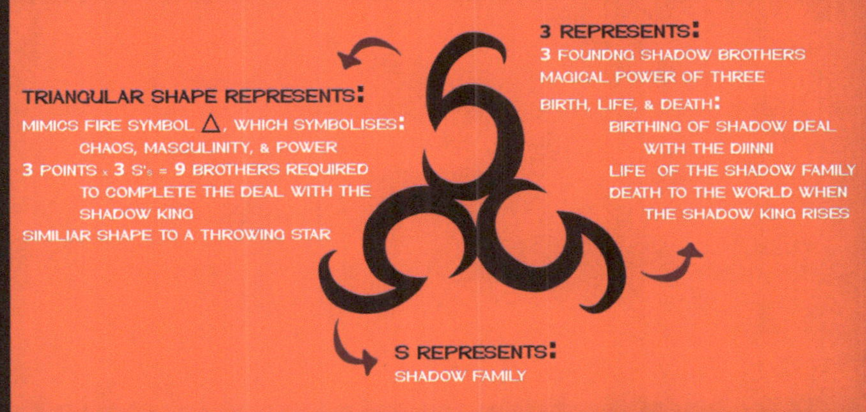

NAME:

Caden Shadow

DOB:
29 December 1895

FAMILY POSITION:
Ex-Boss

INNATE MAGIC:
Telekinesis – specializes in
long-range

*"I will give you the world, Sau.
Let me do this for you. Let me be
your everything."*

Caden Davenport is the firstborn of the Boss of the Red Demons, an infamous gang that used to be based in New York. When it was discovered his innate magic was that of long-range telekinesis, he was forced into an engagement to Sau Shadow when he was thirteen and she was a baby without a name. He tried to refuse, but his father said he'd kill his brothers if he didn't marry and combine their Families.

So Caden named her to show he accepted the engagement, giving her the Drazic word for "defender". He did not see her again until their wedding, but on that day, they were attacked by the Death Hunt, and Sau was taken from him. Her Family was willing to leave her for dead and to pass the firstborn title down to her brother, but Caden demanded that they save her. However, by the time they did, she'd been beaten into a coma, and due to tradition, he could not become Boss of the Shadow Domain until she was with child. So he was forced to breed her while she was under.

Years passed with no change to her condition. The healers eventually told him she was a lost cause. Her own brother tried to kill her to take the throne. But Caden refused to give up on her. He fed her and bathed her with his telekinesis for decades and he read to her every night, ever hopeful that one day she would wake. His brother Myers once asked him why he cared so much when he didn't even know her. He simply replied, "Who else will? Everyone deserves to have someone who will fight for them. Besides, I gave her my word. In sickness and in health, she is mine."

Abused by her family in the name of 'righteousness', Sau Shadow, the firstborn, was brainwashed to be a breeder. She was raised to be obsessed with marrying Caden Davenport. Her mother educated her on how to please a man, and her uncle secretly had her show him what she had learned. Every night, he orally raped her (for she had to stay a virgin) under the disguise of helping her learn how to be a good wife, and due to her upbringing, she believed him without question.

It wasn't until she saw Caden's reaction when he learned what her uncle had done to her that she realised she'd been abused. Slowly, with her husband's help, she learned to unravel all of the shit she'd been taught. However, part of those teachings had been to love Caden wholly and without fault. So she told him she needed to learn who she was without him because she wanted to be able to trust those feelings.

And he loved her enough to walk away.

She is the Reaper of the Sired – one of only seven named sups on Earth, a momma bear to all her children – willing to do whatever it takes to keep them safe, a Boss in her own right despite being a woman – having ruled in Caden's absence until Varius was of age. She is a fighter and a healer, a soldier and a peace-maker, a teacher and a student, and she is blood bonded to Caden... and the lifemate of Aleric Zadar. But she does not kneel to either.

NAME:

VARIUS SIN SHADOW

DOB:
20 November 1988

FAMILY POSITION:
Boss

INNATE MAGIC:
None...

"I don't want you to kill for me, little monster. I want you to live for me! Gods-fucking-dammit, just live for me."

Born as a **witch without magic**, Varius ages and scars like a normal human. Due to this, he has struggled beneath the weight of being a disappointment all his life. His father left when he was twelve because he failed to enter his ascension. His own men have tried to assassinate him multiple times in an attempt to put his brother Leno on the throne. His first crush lured him somewhere private so she and her surprise boyfriend could kill him. So now he keeps everyone at a distance. His paranoia is the only reason he's still alive. **Trust no one.** Regardless of how much he wants to.

Thirteen scars have cut that lesson deep.

But despite this, he will not hesitate to give his life for any of his brothers, especially Rudy, who he practically raised as his own son. He spent many nights fighting his little brother's nightmares so he could sleep in peace. On one of those nights, he got into a fight with a **line-dancing goat** after he refused to learn the choreography of his dance, and it stabbed him in the ass with both horns. Rudy laughed so hard, the goat disappeared, which is the only reason Varius is still alive. Luckily, Sau was able to heal him so he didn't scar.

However, after getting married to Micha Shadow, he is slowly starting to learn how to trust. Emphasis on the slowly.

Leno is the secondborn and a mama's boy. When he was thirteen, he developed a crush on a wolf girl, but then he found out she was already taken. So he got into a fight with her emo girlfriend. She shifted and scratched him across the face from top left to bottom right, blinding him permanently, and that is when he realized he was an idiot. All this time, he'd had a crush on the wrong girl… Now he's determined to find her and marry her – even though he doesn't even know her name.

To help with his blindness, Varius brought home a stray mutt for him. Leno called him Krypto and fell in love with him. Then, much to his mother's horror, he traded thirty of his life years in exchange for sharing three of his dog's senses: sight, touch, and taste. His brothers rib him for this because if he'd chosen sight, hearing, and smell, he'd be a superhero, but being a typical thirteen year old, he was more curious to see if dogs enjoyed having the same meal all the time… and what it felt like to lick one's own dick. Sau was proud of him for accomplishing something so advanced so young, but she told him to *never* use life magic again. Leno promised, but he loves his dog more than anything, so he doesn't care that he will live less because of him.

In the twenty-one years they've been together, they've enjoyed many long walks through the woods and parks, sniffing flowers, and picking up women. Krypto is the *best* wingman, but though Leno enjoys the one-night stands, his heart solely belongs to the wolf girl. And Krypto. Because he's a very, very good boy.

Khalid is the third eldest and the reaper of the Shadow Family. Tasked with killing those who turn traitor, he gives off massive black cat energy. Everyone fears him, even those who love him because they know that that love won't save them if their end is near. He will strike quickly and methodically if it's for the good of the Shadow Family. Due to this, he keeps himself at a distance from everyone.

Everyone except his *kira*.

He gives her every part of him, worshiping her completely because she is the owner of his happiness, the master of his soul. His sun in the world of darkness he lives in. He would do anything for her, whether she asks for it or not. Over-the-top intensity is kind of his MO.

Instead of asking his girl out, he stalked her for two years. Before she even knew they were in a relationship, he blood bonded himself to her – even though she was already his fucking lifemate. He's just so bloody intense, he didn't realise this because he thinks that's just how everyone feels with their special someone.

And when he was forced to beat her, he cut off his left hand because he couldn't bear to know any part of him had hurt her. He is the only brother who can speak magic, so even with one hand, he is still the most dangerous and the most feared.

"Why the fuck aren't we wearing face masks when we're trying to stab each other in the face with swords?"

The laziest and chilliest of the Shadow brothers, Enoch is always trying to find a way to get out of whatever job he's given. If he's challenged to a knife fight, he counters with a gun; fighting "dirty" is not a concept he understands as he only ever fights to win. Otherwise, it's just a "waste of time", and "Ugh, I could be napping right now".

He likes napping, especially in the sunshine. He also likes gaming, which he plays a lot with his twin. He's not very good at it, but as he only plays to peace out, he doesn't care. Plus, Ezriel would've been a professional gamer in another life, so there's really not much point in trying when his brother'll just carry him to victory.

The only thing he puts true effort in is his relationship with Stormie Green. Ever since she punched him in the nose for pulling her hair in the first grade, he's been crushing on her *hard*. He apologised by giving her a rock during recess, and they've been good friends ever since. He asked her out in high school, but she turned him down. They're still friends though as he respects her as a person rather than just as a potential lover. However, since then, he's only dated a few times, and the only time he has sex is when Ezriel drags him into a threesome, but he's never put his heart into it, not seeing the point of trying when he already knows who he wants to wed.

Over a decade later, the two of them are now engaged – a political arrangement. But he's hopeful it can turn into something more.

The twins always celebrated their birthdays together due to obvious reasons. But when Ezriel was eleven, he found out that he'd actually been born a whole twenty-three minutes later – after midnight. Feeling utterly betrayed that all this time they'd only been celebrating Enoch's birthday, Ez demanded that the next eleven birthdays be on his date. Enoch called him dumb and told him they should demand to have separate birthdays now that the secret was out, and he quickly agreed.

Bemused, Sau apologised for not having kept track of the time during her gruelling, twenty-five hour labour that caused her to rip her vagina to her ass. They told her "ew", and then Ez said he should get a computer for having suffered through the last eleven false-birthdays and that story. So she got him a state-of-the-art gaming computer that year, and from that moment on, he got hooked on gaming. If he wasn't part of the Family, he could very easily go pro in a variety of games.

Despite being a geek and a gamer though, he's also a ladies' boy and a freak in the sheets, using his telekinesis to control multiple toys at once. If he's with a person for long enough (years as biomass is harder to work with), he can study their atomic make-up to the point he can control their body – and their O.

As with all identical twins, their magic grows when they're together, which is why he's constantly getting Enoch to join him in threesomes. He gets to be a lot freakier.

Acheon Shadow runs the legit business side of the Family: the hotels, landscaping, butchers, docks, etc, as well as the Floridian network of drugs (Ricks and Vs). Due to him having his 'talons' in everything, Maddox nicknamed him Talon when he was a kid, and he's gone by that name ever since, so much so that even Sau calls him it – unless he's in trouble.

Despite the treaty between the three gangs though, he's killed a lot of Blood Fang members. In high school, he fell in love with a blood bank – a morsel for the vamps to feed on whenever they liked. Her name was Jackie, and she dreamed of being an astronaut even though she knew she wouldn't live long enough to go to college. He was determined, however, to save her. He eventually got her to accept to go on a date with him, where he took her to see a meteor shower on the beach and gave her a ring he made, inlaid with a real meteorite.

However, when he went back to his car to get more drinks, he came back to find she'd been attacked. A group of unknown vamps had beaten her and drained her dry, then painted "witch whore" on her forehead with her own blood. She died in his arms. Now the only time he fucks is at Death Hunt brothels – nothing but sexual release. His heart will forever be hers, though he often develops soft spots for those who are in trouble, wanting to be the white knight he failed to be when he was a teen.

Rudy Mitchell Shadow

DOB:
31 October 1997

FAMILY POSITION:
Cleaner

INNATE MAGIC:
Chaos Magic –
Turns Fears into Reality

"Love isn't weak, you idiot. Needing you wasn't a weakness of mine. It allowed me to grow strong."

Despite being the strongest Shadow brother, Rudy has an aversion to violence. He's the only good person in the family, hating to see anyone or anything suffer. To him, a life is a life, regardless of whether it's a kitten or a human, and he'd spend just as much time helping a little critter than he would a child. When he was five, he brought home his first hurt stray in order to nurse it back to health – but alas, it was a possum. And it was dead.

Due to his kind nature, he rarely joins his Family in fights. Instead, he comes in after to do the cleaning up, which he does while listening to music and dancing with the body parts. As his innate magic forces him to see everyone's greatest fears whenever he gets too close, he prefers to be with the dead rather than the living. For the same reason, he also enjoys driving through the countryside on his own and, on the rare occasions he gets to, sailing out to sea on his boat, which is called *Whale Endowed*.

Born mute, he is the reason everyone in the family knows sign language, and they use it as the default language whenever he's present. However, Maddox often turns out the lights just to "shut him up", much to Rudy's annoyance.

A lover of life and living, he takes pleasure in the little things and stops to smell the roses. He also picked out Maddox's middle name. As Varius likes bugs, so Rudy has fond memories of them, and he thought "Snail" was a great choice for a name.

Maddox is, quite frankly, a little shit. When he's torturing someones's fiance to get them to break, he actually has the nerve to ask them out because, "You're going to be single soon, so what do you say? You like the ballet?" He constantly goads his brothers, and if he had Rudy's magic, he would absolutely be terrorising them all the time. This is why he often smells like onions too – Sau and Micha constantly throw them at his head for being purposefully annoying.

Despite his big dick energy though, he actually has the smallest (soft: 3", hard: 6") in the family. However, he damn well knows how to use it, his tongue, his fingers, toys, and psychological torture to get his girl off. Obviously, his favourite thing to do is edging because he's an ass.

He's the smartest Shadow brother too and the only one who's been to uni, having graduated with a degree in psychology, which he uses to torture people – and to get into their head when he shapeshifts into them. Due to this, everyone but his brothers try to avoid him as it only takes him a few minutes to study their DNA enough to become a clone of them – shorter still if all he wants to take is their face.

He loves the ballet and screaming metal, and he's fiercely protective of his family. Despite his joking and annoying nature, he is always serious when they need him to be.

Micha lost her childhood at age eleven. Her mom died when she was giving birth to her sister, Lou, and her father spiralled into an all-consuming grief, effectively causing her to lose both her parents at once as well as forcing her to become the mom her sister needed as her older brothers were too busy with being assassins.

A few years later, her father mentioned the prospect of marriage to her. Terrified she'd be forced to leave Lou, Micha chose to become an assassin – even though she had little interest in it and just wanted to be a singer.

She was trained brutally by her father, more so than any of the other kids as he tried to scare her off from this life. What remained of their relationship crumbled into one of hatred and pain. But her stubborn nature saw her excelling at the top of her class, and all that remained as a 'hurdle' to her training was her compassion. So for her first mission, she was sent to a child's beauty pageant that was known for gang members using it as a hunting ground – both for sex trafficking and brides.

In her naivety, she thought she'd been hired to save a child from that life, but in fact, she'd been hired to get rid of the number one girl – a ten-year-old called Bambi. So she came up with a way to fake her death, but her client wanted her to disfigure her face instead. And once a Black takes a job, the only way out of it is through death. This is one of Micha's heaviest guilts. Bambi killed herself a year later.

As a kid, Scarlett loved learning. She discovered books at nineteen months and was rarely seen without one. She slept with them, ate with them, even bathed with them. By the age of six, she was reading *1984* by George Orwell. At ten, she was planning how to get into Harvard or Yale. But then came puberty. At twelve, she moved to St. Augustine, Florida, and she developed size D breasts. The boys at her new school "accidentally" kept spilling water on her, and the teachers blamed her for being a distraction. So her love for learning turned into severe anxiety, and she developed an eating disorder in an attempt to make her body less desirable/"distracting". Her mother's attempt to "help" only hurt her more, and so she rarely left her room.

But she likes to watch true crime and loves to dance when no one's looking. She writes in her diary every night like clockwork, and she has a dark sense of humour.

It wasn't until she met Khalid at twenty-two, though, that she learned to love herself for who she was. She's now learning how to use a wand and to summon demons. She's also starting to get into fighting shape so she can help protect her *kira*. He does not tease her for this; he simply helps her accomplish her goal. And so the demons won't ever know her real name, she's changed it to Kiyana.

She never knew her dad, having been conceived on a one-night stand, but he was an Atlantean – a race hunted by the gods; she has a half-sister called Charlie Markson.

NAME:

Stormie Shadow

DOB:

21 June 1991

FAMILY POSITION:
Soldier's Wife

INNATE MAGIC:
Shielding

"Aw, you want to know my bodycount? Which one? And are we counting bodies I just helped hide or those I actively helped die?"

Born into the Shadow Domain Family, Stormie always knew what her future held – to be married and bred in order to increase the number of witches in St. Augustine. When she hit her ascension and was shown to be a shielder, however, Sau Shadow sent her away to study her craft. If she got strong enough, she would be able to contain Varius if his curse ever broke free, and Sau liked to have multipe back-up plans in place.

She was brought back to marry Enoch – a boy she'd only ever seen as a friend. Sau gave her the option to decline, but she knew he would treat her well and that a good marriage was often built on friendship. She just didn't expect all her old feelings for Ezriel to come rushing back as soon as she saw him.

Six years ago, before she had left to study under a master shielder in Asia, she had poured her heart out to him, but Ezriel had turned her down, telling her he would never hurt his brother like that – even if he did return her feelings. They never spoke of it again, and their friendship became strained. She tried to move on by dating multiple men and a few women over the years. She nearly succeded at one point, nearly becoming engaged to him, but he cheated on her with her best friend.

Knowing the agony of being cheated on, Stormie will never act on her feelings for Ezriel. But the happy marriage she thought she could have now seems impossible.

NAME:

MARRABELLE

DOB:
Unknown

FAMILY POSITION:
Maddox's 'Pet' / Best Friend / Lover

INNATE MAGIC:
None

"You should've seen how Varius fucked her, Maddox. His dick was so big, and they did it right on your bed. Oooh! Ask them to come back. Please?"

Marrabelle is a **sex-fiend** who was born in a happiness cult on Brownston, Gaera. Having been brainwashed to be **perpetually happy** ever since she was born, she does not know how to process anything else. She is never sad or angry or anything other than horny or happy. She never tells anyone no, and she always tries to cheer other people up in fear because she's afraid they'll get **arrested for being sad** (as it's illegal where she's from). She also talks about sex. A lot.

At some point, she volunteered to be an **Inviter** – a person who left on a quest to invite everyone in all the Seven Planes to an orgy in her home town. This was an honourable position, and despite having just given birth to a daughter, Marrabelle left for work, knowing she'd never return to see her girl grow up. As Brownston was a cult family where everyone took care of everyone, however, she knew her daughter would be in "good" hands – too brainwashed to know that **free use** without an age restriction was not a good thing. It happened to her and everyone she knew; she did not know anything different. Her daughter's name is **Fabia**.

When she arrived on Earth, she asked Maddox if he wanted to attend an orgy. He said no and kidnapped her instead. However, not knowing fear or any of her own desires – only ever the desire to make someone else happy, she willingly stays as his pet. He is slowly teaching her what it means to be her own person, though, and undoing the **brainwashing** of her past.

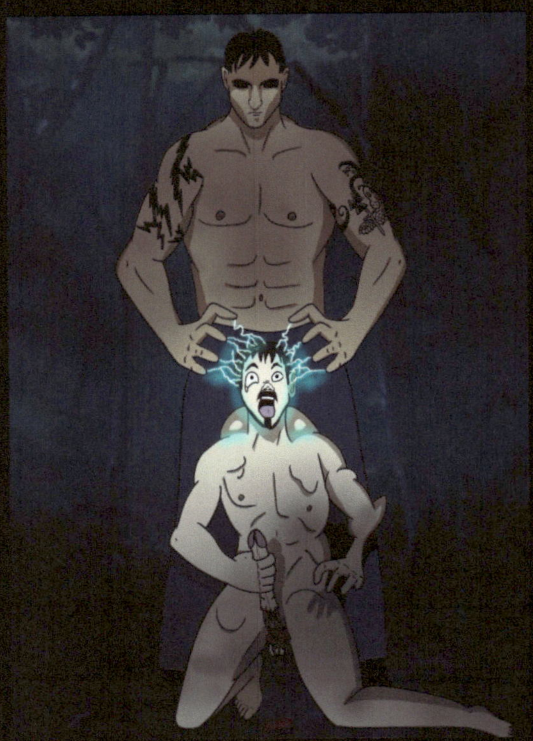

His father was a serial killer who liked to torture his victims. His mother was one of those women, lured over to his house after she "lost" her dog and he "found" it. He raped her for months, and once she got pregnant, he "helped" her give birth by opening her up without any pain relief. Although he planned to beat her to death with the baby, she convinced him to keep their child as a pet.

Dayne lived in a dog cage, with a front row seat to the rape and further torture of his mom and the other victims. He was fed dog food and given no bed to sleep on. A shock collar stayed on him at all times, and his cage was rarely cleaned of his filth. His mom finally died when he was seven, and his father planned to kill him after his ascension as a sacrifice in a dark spell.

But Micha and Stefaan Black found him when he was ten and she was twelve. His father hadn't been around for days, presumably killed by the SCU. Dayne was so hungry, he tried to eat her, but she convinced her father to let her bring him home anyway. She taught him to read and write and gave him a tattoo to let him know she would always be there for him – she claims it's a bunny, but it's really just a dick. When he hit his ascension, he gave her one too–a smiley face with a dick for a nose.

He specialises in shaping the electricity in one's brain. With both of his hands on their head, he can control their body. He and Micha became an assassin duo.

NAME:

"THE SHADOW KING"

DOB:
Unknown

FAMILY POSITION:
To be decided...

INNATE MAGIC:
OP Shadow Daddy

"Let's make a deal. You shut the fuck up and die, and I will be forever thankful."

One of the major players in the war against the gods, the Shadow King was locked away in a secret prison that was guarded by a pack of hellhounds. One day, he managed to break free, and he raced through the Seven Planes with the demon dogs and a group of gods hot on his trail. Knowing his sister, the Queen of Darkness, was imprisoned in the Plane of Monsters, he headed for that world, hoping he could get her out. Together, they would have a chance at starting Ragnarok and ending the gods once and for all.

Alas, an arrow from Artemis' bow cut him down, and knowing he would not reach her prison in time, he shadow-walked, stepping directly into the shadow of the closest human – a man by the name of Diega Ominara who was searching this plane for his wife. With him, he made a deal: he'd give him the ability to walk safely through this plane, as well as the power to shift into and create magical shadows.

In exchange, Diega would gift him the ninth consecutive brother of his bloodline.

The deal was struck. The Shadow King was caught. He was taken back to his prison, where the spells containing him and the hellhounds watching him were increased a thousandfold. But he knows it's only a matter of time before his deal sets him free. For when the ninth brother is born, he will not simply receive it as a sacrifice. He will step into the baby's body and claim it as his.

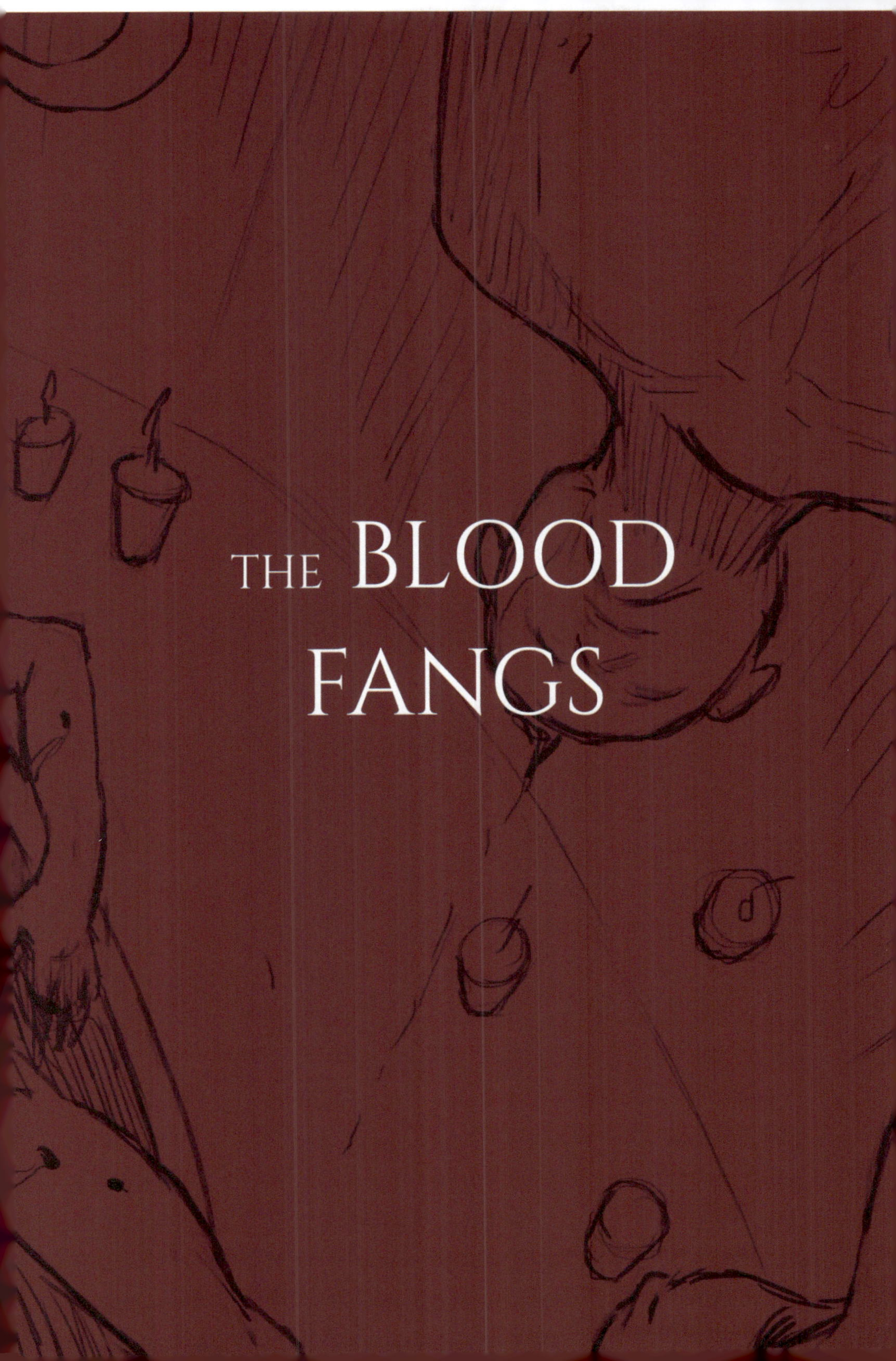
THE BLOOD
FANGS

Three and a half thousand years ago, Sebastian the Ancient Destroyer and Rakian the Rise of Ragnarok waged war across the Seven Planes. They destroyed Persic and slaughtered many of the primoridial elementals that kept the plane of Gaera alive, throwing it into decay. When they came to Earth with their army, they had the main goal of taking Atlantis – an advanced kingdom full of the brightest minds in all of the Seven Planes and housing thousands of advanced weaponry and technology. Specially, however, they sought the *Scrolls of Atlantis*.

Crifton Renegair was a soldier of theirs, having only passed his ascension a few years previous. Despite his young age, he slaughtered his way across the battlefields and within a few years, he grew a name for himself, rising in rank until he became a Lakothar – a general who was allowed to sire.

With his legion of infamous vampires, known as the Blood Fangs, he spearheaded a siege on Atlantis. However, unlike the previous attempts to take the kingdom, his actually succeeded. He and his soldiers fought their way past an army of chimeras (the humanoid experiments, not the creatures) and made it into the heart of Atlantis.

Once inside, Crifton was gravely wounded. But still he fought on for glory and kingdom and because he believed in Sebastian's message: "the gods have failed us; it is time to become our own gods". He and his army pushed further and further inside.

In a last drastic measure, the Atlantians sank the entirety of their kingdom, composing of various connected islands, into the sea. The *Scrolls of Atlantis*, the book that gave them the knowledge to create chimeras, was lost forever, and Crifton, who was in the heart of their main island when the explosions went off, died.

Or so everyone believed. In truth, he managed to phase away at the last second. Too wounded to control where he went, he landed in the middle of a random field, then promptly passed out from blood loss.

When he woke, he found himself chained to a tree, with a group of children ranging from toddlers to teenagers glaring at him. He tried to phase himself free, but the chain on his wrist was a witch's snare, and it kept him restrained. A woman barely much older than the kids, grubby and carrying a small clay pot in her hands, sent the others away. Then she sat down on the grass beside him and cut her wrist. She only gave him a few drops of blood, just enough to keep him from dying.

They didn't share a language – she was Timucua as he'd landed in the area that is now present day St Augustine. She knew not who he was, but she recognised his armour as being that of the enemy – Sebastian's war having waged across the entire world. In miming and broken words, she told him she was fattening him up as a sacrifice to the spirits. They normally took children, but she thought they would be pleased with a man who had fought alongside the invaders. With a man who had helped rape their land and slaughter their people.

However, at some point, the two of them fell in love, and he left Sebastian's army to stay with her – and all the orphans she'd "collected" as a surrogate mother.

But the Shadow Domain, a gang of witches and werewolves, was fully established in the area. They demanded payment, and he refused. After they killed the woman and many of his children, he created a rival gang. He called them the Blood Fangs, and he embraced the soldier he used to be before *she* had tamed the beast.

Initiation Ritual

The initiate is beaten by a gang of members for two minutes. If they survive, they are welcomed. If not, their body is taken out to sea. Weapons can be used.

Sometimes, initiates are just flat-out murdered, but most of the time, they are "lightly" beaten (heavy bruises and maybe one broken bone rather than multiple broken ones) with the purpose of welcoming them into the gang.

Blood Fangs Symbol

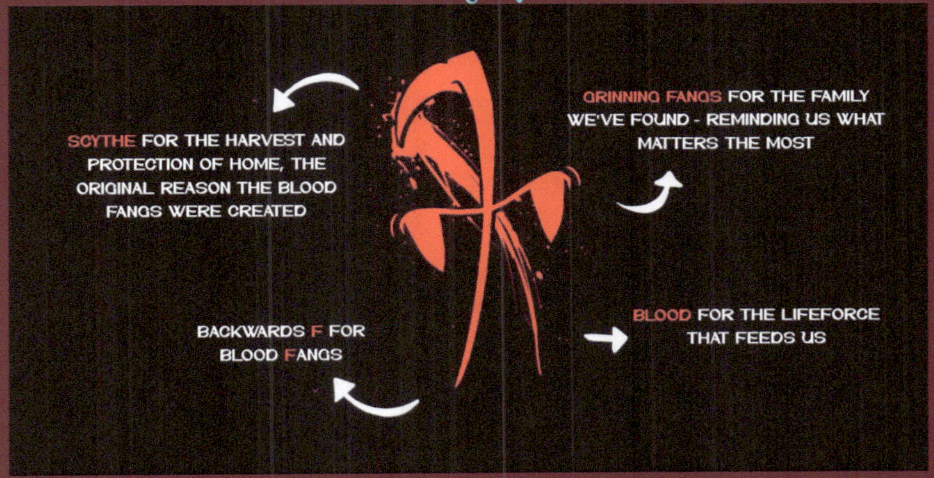

Blood Fangs Ranking

Boss – leader of the gang; the only one who's allowed to sire

Underboss – second-in-command; the one the rest of the gang brings their issues to

Capo – No human can be a capo. They are either born or sired vampires.

Soldier – Born vampires are ranked higher than the sired and both are ranked higher than Earthers, but all are given jobs to do by the capos. Not all of them know about the existence of vampires.

Feeder – They find bloodbanks. They have more prestige than soldiers given how 'important' their job is, but they aren't ranked any higher.

Dirty Cop – They're more associates rather than full gang members, but they're still treated with more respect than a bloodbank.

Bloodbank – Human who is passed around like a tray of hors d'oeuvres. They can be Earthers or lower vamps. They are technically a part of the gang and so they have the protection of the gang, but they are treated like utter shit and they rarely live longer than a few years.

A **charming** asshole.

Not only does he love to **whistle** while he's torturing people, but he also likes to tell them dad jokes. How he's managed to live this long, having annoyed every person he's ever met, is this series' greatest mystery.

But only a fool would underestimate him or forget how dangerous he is when he wants to be. He might be a prankster, but his idea of "funny" is giving a girl a knife and laughing as she tries to stab him. Then he fucks her to death, breaking her pelvis against the wall. Or he rips off her head while she's giving him head. The only lady he hasn't **killed during sex** recently is Sau Shadow. But who knows how long that will last?

A bonafide psychopath, Aleric is a true wild card. Once, he even turned a merchant into a vampire simply because he liked the sauce he'd made, and he didn't want to lose access to it as the years passed. He treats the entre world and everyone in it as his toys to play with, and he 100% channels a little girl's soul as he does so, pulling off Barbie limbs and tossing around their heads.

He loves to play *Mario*, and he can play the **violin** professionally. But what he really likes to do is torture people in his special torture chair that faces his bed.

Given Vlad is way more levelheaded than his Boss, a *lot* of people want him to kill Aleric and take his throne. He does 90% of the Boss stuff anyway, as well as runs their network of dirty cops (he simply phases if he's needed for Blood Fangs work). But though some days he is sorely tempted to kill the guy who's the biggest pain in his ass, he never will. Because he knows he can't. Aleric claims he's three hundred years old... but he's been saying that ever since Vlad met him back in 1915.

Born in Alaska, Vlad arrived in St. Augustine because Destiny, his younger sister (though the oldest of the girls) was marrying Colton, the son of Aleric Zadar. After her death, he stayed to get revenge on the Shadow family. However, when Sau forced a peace treaty between the three gangs, he honoured it for the good of his people. Until he met Rudy Shadow.

As soon as they locked eyes, he instantly knew they were lifemates. Vlad's hatred of the Shadow family runs deep though, and he refuses to let anything real develop between them. They've fucked a few times, but that stopped once they were caught by the reaper. Rudy asked him out after their two Families became allies, but Vlad showed up to their date smelling like an orgy, having only agreed to come so he could hurt him.

It is one of his biggest regrets.

THE DEATH HUNT

They were originally part of the Shadow Domain when they first came through the portal, and it is because of the Shadow witches that these werewolves (not all wolves) are able to eat a member of their pack and retain a bit of their power.

However, the gang eventually split due to their differences after Earth was cut off from the rest of the Seven Planes. The werewolves felt their culture was being erased now that they couldn't step back to Blódyrió whenever the mood struck, and as Artemis' moon was a source of their power, they slowly weakened over time. This led to them being second-class citizens, and it eventually all came to a head when Olesia D'treesic, the Underboss at the time, spurred a coup against her Boss and lover, Rivan Shadow.

The battle was bloody, and with the Blood Fangs joining in to kill them all, the Shadow Domain barely survived. In the aftermath, the gang split into two. The witches kept their original name, whereas the werewolves called themselves the Death Hunt.

Death Hunt Alpha Challenge

The Boss of the Death Hunt is always a born werewolf – though male or female doesn't mater, and they can be challenged at any time. The winner is decided when one wolf is either killed or chased off with their tails between their legs. If the latter, the whole pack chases them down in their wolf forms, so they rarely get away alive.

Death Hunt Symbol

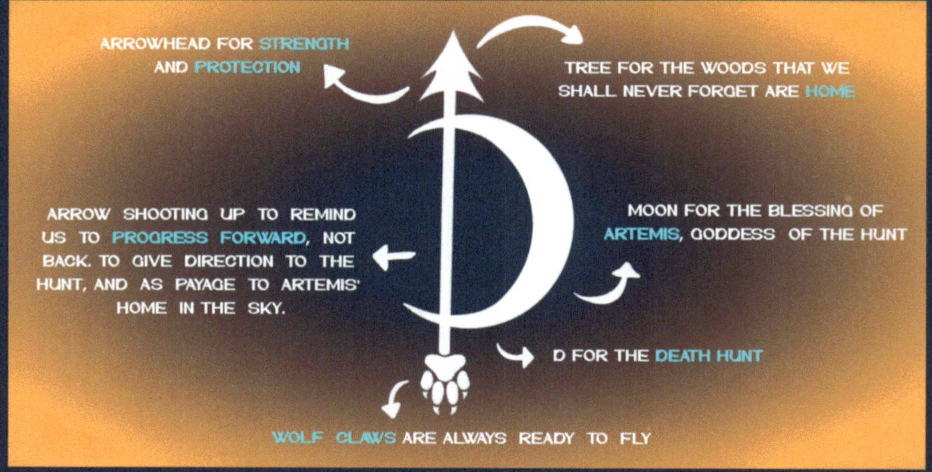

Death Hunt Initiation

As the spilling of blood ties the pack together, the initiate is kidnapped by a group of Death Hunt members and then taken to the middle of the woods, where they will be chased with knives or claws.

If the initiate is a human, they will be given a dummy knife and let loose in the woods. They'll then be chased by around a dozen human members, who have actual knives. If they manage to escape their pursuers for an hour, then they can join the gang without being stabbed.

If the initiate is a werewolf, either bitten or born, they are chased in their human form all night by members in their wolf forms. If they evade capture, they're allowed to join without being mauled to near death. How well they fight back will tell the pack where they belong in rank. Although there are only three wolf positions: alpha (ruling party – normally one with a mate, sometimes poly), beta, and omega, the hierarchy within the beta camp is fiercly established.

Hybrid Breeding Program

In an attempt to power himself up enough to be able to enter the Underworld to get his mate back, Antonio has turned the Death Hunt into a breeding program for hybrids. He started it when Sau disappeared after becoming Reaper of the Sired. At first, he only used volunteers – lower betas that wanted to climb the ranks. They were bred constantly and with multiple partners as he tried to figure out the right combinations that would birth him hybrids.

However, as they are extremely rare, this took a very long time, and so he started forcing the lower members of his gang to participate. This eventually spread to him forcing every female in his Family. He would breed them with hundreds of partners for a year, aborting any children who weren't hybrids. At the end of the year, if they couldn't get pregnant with a hybrid, they were kicked out of the program, though they still stayed within the Family. If they were capable of creating hybrids, then they had their every whim catered to. They rose to the top level of betas, and they often turned into fucking divas.

For the last few months, he's been kidnapping male born vampires from the Blood Fangs and forcing them to breed with his women. Unfortunately, due to a werewolf's cum and saliva being venomous to vampires, the vampires all end up dying a very gruesome and agonising death, where their skin and organs all melt and turn into goo.

Antonio has also tried to create hybrids in a lab by employing a mad healer. He has been unable to create true hybrids but has created a half dozen chimeras, which are faster, stronger, and have more grotesque animal forms. However, they become infertile.

"Smile for me, little hellfire. Just one more time."

Born with golden eyes and hair, his parents feared he was sun-touched – seen as a curse amongst werewolves, who are blessed by Artemis' moon. They believed if they didn't make his life miserable, then his curse of misery would pass on to them. So although they didn't beat him, they left him to cry as a pup, only ever feeding him, never soothing him once. As he aged, they continued to ignore him while favouring their other children. They never paid for his hobbies or supported his achievements, and the whole pack ostricized him, though he never became an omega due to being able to shift the fastest in the pack. Due to being sun-touched, he could also shift without being completely at the mercy of those around him.

But then he met Siome (he 12; she 10), and his whole world changed. She was a defiant child who didn't listen to her parents about staying away from the cursed child. She ignored his grumpiness and his attempts to scare her off, of which there were plenty. As the years passed, however, her infectuous energy and constant optimism started to grow on him, and they became childhood sweethearts.

But scared of his curse killing her, he ended up sending her away when she was eighteen. He didn't see her for another eighty-seven years, but as soon as he did, their chemistry exploded, and they spent every waking moment with each other. Alas, only days after he proposed to her, she was killed. He's determined to bring her back to life by sacrificing the Shadow Family. He's changed his middle name to hers.

She's the grandchild of Antonio Garcia, but she's not actually related to him. Her grandfather was some loner wolf the female alpha of their pack (her grandma and pack mate to Antonio after Siome died) had an affair with for a few months.

Zita's always been a spirited child – a bit too troublesome for her parents. However, she never really got in trouble with the pack at all until her family caught the eye of Antonio's double (who stood in for Antonio from time to time in an attempt to foil any assassination attempts as well as hide his movements from the Death Hunt and Shadow Domain as he moved the pieces on his chessboard – in a game the other two gangs didn't even know they were playing until it was too late).

He fucked her mom and her older sister, Abril, and he tried to fuck her too when she was sixteen. When she rejected him by scratching his face, he raped her, then used his power to force her into the role of omega. As the rest of the pack wasn't aware Antonio even had a double, they simply thought they were obeying his orders.

Due to her defiant nature, she is often beaten and severely bullied. She has dozens of scars on her back and limbs due to pack members beating and abusing her.

The position of omega is held for life. There's rarely ever been a case of one rising back up to a beta, but Zita is deteremined to join that very small number.

THE OTHER
PLAYERS

Blacks

Their Boss is Stefaan Black, and they are a Family of assassins who were recently given territory by the Shadow Domain in exchange for Micha's hand in marriage. They are based in Tennessee and are available for hire by anyone. Once a contract is signed, it cannot be broken except in death – either theirs, their target, or the idiot who tried to cancel it. Death before thirty is common. Retirement is a rarity.

Goodbye World –the best hacker group in the world, made up of three women: Mickyla Hatch, Kati Vosika, Ashley Quiett– is also a part of the Black Family.

Special Crimes Unit

The SCU is a world-renowned private agency that helps local police forces and government agencies solve 'impossible crimes'. They are often in the news because of this. However, their real purpose is to govern the sups on Earth. They are a branch of the Elv've'Nor, an interplanal organisation that polices the Seven Planes and which has direct ties to the archangels.

So they only take on cases they suspect might be related to sups killing Earthers. They also meet with any sup that has been charged with a crime to make sure they can be held for the term of their sentence without revealing their true nature. If not, they will either fake their death or organise a false transfer and take them away.

Their prison is hidden deep in an undersea base, and no one has ever escaped from it before. In edition to having cells that can hold even a werewolf under the Craving, they work like a well-oiled machine, know every race's weaknesses, and have a lot of tech and magical items that can really fuck people up. These were gathered from the ruins of Atlantis before the kingdom fell during the Great Extinction. So not even Aleric Zadar likes to call their attention – especially as they can transfer prisoners off-world to places like Damaculus – a prison where only the worst of the worst end up.

Due to being undermanned, however, the SCU mostly ignores sups that only hurt other sups. This is why they haven't been to St Augustine for decades.

Warriors Against Lycans and Lessers

They started from a right-wing militia that came across a werewolf. They tortured and then butchered the kid for being 'unholy' and 'illegal', and then they went out to hunt for more. They didn't find another one for years, but then they came across a family in the woods who were Black, and "Black people don't like camping, so that's sus", and they killed them, believing they were werewolves. They weren't, but reason means little in the face of racism.

Eventually, their numbers expanded, and now they have chapters all across the USA. Their ranks are mostly filled with white men, with only 12% of their members being women and 3% of them being a minority race.

They work behind the scenes, not trusting the government to get things done. So they're targeting politicians and cops in an attempt to pull them into their circle and get them to create local task forces they can infiltrate/control so they can go hunting for "the greatest threat to America".

Ashley Mattos, a succubi, and her twin brother, Aaron Mattos, an incubi, are the creators of Ricks and Vs. These sex potions change one's anatomy to be "more fun" (extra G-spot and clit, vibrating dick, adds ridges, tongues, hooks, or even a second dick, grows dick, tightens pussy, etc) and heightens the pleasure of an orgasm. The potions themselves aren't addicting, but experiencing the effect of them is.

Their drug empire rakes in billions a year even though they are notoriously strict about who they sell to and who is allowed to distribute for them in an attempt to protect their brand. Each partner must agree to kill any unauthorised trader, so if anyone tries to sell a vial without permission, they will instantly have a multi-billion dollar bounty on their heads, and nowhere on Earth will be safe to hide.

Vs that increase the chance of pregnancy are illegal due to them requiring a fertile womb and a set of testicles to make. The Mattos twins are heavily wanted by the SCU.

SUPERNATURAL HUMANS

Long ago, there were a *lot* of wars. Titans were fighting gods. Frost giants were fighting gods. Gods were fighting gods. Gods were teaming up with titans and frost giants and other factions to fight other gods – until there was one giant fucking war that raged across the universe, leading to the annihilation of nearly everything.

Eventually, all that remained were the "good guys" (because history's always written by the good guys), and this included the djinn, Graecian gods, Vanir gods, Aesir gods, and the Gaelic gods. Everyone else either got murdered or imprisoned in the jails of the gods, also known as black holes.

So then there was peace.

Until the gods backstabbed the djinn, of course.

But *then* there was real peace.

And then there came boredom.

And then there came restlessness and weapons ready to strike.

Fearing another war, Hera, Freya, and the Morrighan decided to ease tensions by creating the Panhellenic Games. Consisting of four rounds, they allowed the gods to take out their frustrations and love for violence in 'friendly' competitions. They take place every 10,000 years, and one of these rounds consists of a team of three or less creating a human. These humans are placed into an arena full of monsters, then they fight to the death until only one remains. Afterwards, the winner is taken to a new world (one of the Seven Planes), and more of their kind is created so they may populate and prosper.

And so the era of humans (any creature made in the image of a god) was born.

The first winners were the angels. Then the drazic demons, etc, etc. The winners of these games are known as champion races, and they all have the primal urge to compete and win crafted into their DNA. Sometimes these races evolve into new ones, known as transhift races, such as when an angel falls from grace and turns into an eknor demon or when cubi (succubi and incubi) evolve enough to give birth to an empath. The first family of champion and transhift races are both called primordials.

When two different races get together, their offspring normally comes out as the stronger parent. However, this is not a guarantee due to various genetic factors, and so it isn't uncommon for a mix couple to have a mixture of offspring. Sometimes, they can even birth a zilcher, which is when the magical genes of both parents cancel each other out. These are not hybrids because they are not, for instance, getting the upper half of a centaur and the bottom half of a minotaur. They are simply non-magical. These humans have an average lifespan of thirty-two years –

eighty-eight if they live in a community of zilchers (due to their inability to heal, their lack of strength, speed, and durability, and their dulled senses, they accidentally get killed a lot by other humans).

Now, hybrids are the opposite of zilchers. Instead of the magical genes of their parents canceling each other out, they amplify each other significantly, creating a human that is on par power-wise with a demi-god (though some are on par with a descendant – a child of the gods (as titans birth gods, gods birth descendants)). They are extremely rare as most humans can never birth a hybrid due to their genes, but hybrids are greatly feared and ostracised. They are normally hunted down in the womb and killed before they can be born. Their mothers are usually slaughtered too. All hybrids are infertile.

At some point in time, the zilchers were moved to Earth. Then when the Great Extinction took place (a war that raged across the Seven Planes for a thousand-odd years), the portals to Earth were closed by decree of the archangels, and they forgot from whence they came. Well, most of them.

Due to this though, they get confused when you tell them the rest of the creatures are also humans, so the term 'supernaturals' or 'sup' was created to make it easier for them to distinguish between themselves and other humans created in the gods' images. Earth humans are sometimes called Earthers.

However, some Earthers also think supernatural humans include monsters, but this is *not* true. Monsters are completely different because they were not made in the image of a god. Now, some of them are capable of shifting into a humanoid shape due to a blessing bestowed upon them by a god at a later date, but they treat it more like a costume they really don't want to wear.

Monsters	Humans
✔ **Don't** have a humanoid shape*	✔ Have a humanoid shape
✔ Like to eat and kill humans	✔ Like to kill humans but not eat*
✔ Live in nature	✔ Live in houses
✔ Can't breed with any humans**	✔ Can breed with all humans
✔ Don't self-heal	✔ Self-heal**
✔ Weren't created by the gods	✔ Were created by the gods
✔ Not affected by the Craving	✔ Can be affected by the Craving
✔ Die of old age	✔ With age comes increased power
*unless gifted to them by the gods **can still fuck them	*unless they're cannibals **unless they're zilchers

All humans are susceptible to the effects of the Craving (a mindless, animalistic frenzy), but the werewolves, vampires, and berserkers are the most at risk due to their increased blood lust. As well as all those who are over a thousand years old – as this is the time when the brain starts to fracture over too many memories and experiences.

Archangels

After a vicious win in the first ever Panhellenic Games, the angel Varachiel was in need of a home. After much debate and design, her two creators – Freya, the Aesir Goddess of Love and Magic, and Odin, the Aesir God of War and Wisdom, crafted the world Halzaja. They populated it with more of her kind, then left them to their own devices.

Ten thousand years later, the second Panhellenic Games were held, and a new winner emerged victorious. He was a drazic demon called Lucifer, created by the Three Furies.

The two races waged war, neither knowing another species to be friendly given the brutality of the games. The drazics carved out their home on the east side of Halzaja, calling their domain Volskera, while the angels claimed the west, calling it Hevana.

One day, a drazic child called Nathasa ventured into Hevana. She was found by Varachiel and returned home by the angel queen herself. Genuinely happy to see his niece unharmed, Lucifer invited his greatest enemy to stay the night as to trek all the way back to Hevana immediately would be dangerous. Planning to slit his throat while he slept and thus end this war once and for all, Varachiel agreed.

But she did not slit his throat that night.

Determined to end this war as well, Lucifer proposed they marry and unite their lands.

Varachiel eventually agreed.

Their reign was a rocky one – neither having experienced trust. Both of their people tried to assassinate the other ruler, and one of them nearly succeeded. As Varachiel held a dying Lucifer in her arms, she prayed to her creator Freya:

"Spare him, Oh Great Goddess, and I will lead your armies to the end of time."

Lucifer was healed on the brink of death, and in exchange, a hundred of the best angel warriors will serve Freya as Valkyries, there to be called upon when Ragnarok eventually rises.

Struck by the show of Varachiel's and Lucifer's love for each other, the angels and demons eventually accepted their push for peace. For thirteen years, they enjoyed life without pain, but it was not a future meant to last.

Every time Varachiel became pregnant, their kingdom rejoiced, and a month-long celebration was had throughout all of Halzaja. Holidays were created after each one, but on the birth of their eighth child, a girl, Freya and Odin decided to visit.

The Aesir God of War and Wisdom took one look at them with his all-seeing eye and immediately attacked. For their children were neither angels nor demons. They were hybrids – and their ninth child would hail the arrival of Ragnarok.

It was only because of Freya's intervention that they survived that day.

"What comes will come. You know we cannot twist the strings of fate.
Let us not kill the Valkyries who are to serve us when Ragnarok rises."

But Odin was not satisfied. So he split them apart forever.

The angels were forced to live only in the sky, and the demons were forced below the earth. Then the beautiful terrain was set ablaze, never to be inhabited again.

Lucifer lost his freedom trying to stay with Varachiel. She would have fought to stay with him too, but Freya had already claimed her soul as hers. Now bound to the goddess until the end of days, Varachiel cannot disobey her.

With their family and kingdom destroyed, the eight children vowed to one day grow strong enough to stand against the gods and reunite their mother and father.

But with age, came wisdom, and the archangels soon learned that overthrowing them would trigger Ragnarok. And so they turned their attention to protecting the Seven Planes. It is they who police the gods and uphold the balance of the worlds.

During one of their missions though, they were forced to kill their little sister, and that forever changed them. Too vicious and cold, they have started to forget what it means to be human.

ARCHANGELS – FEARED EVEN MORE THAN THE GODS

1. *Michael* – the Enforcer of Balance, the Destroyer of Good and Evil. With the weight of the world on his shoulders, he cannot falter.
2. *Gabriel* – the Holder of Chaos. Uptight, but beneath his harsh exterior... lies a freak.
3. *Raphael* – the Giver of Pleasure and the Taker of Pain; the Giver of Pain and the Taker of Pleasure. A hard and soft dom all rolled into one.
4. *Beliel* – the Bringer of Light.
5. *Azrael* – the Bringer of Death. Rumors say his tattoos house the souls of all he's slain, trapping them for all eternity against his skin, and they shove each other aside in their soundless screams as they try to get out.
6. *Raguel* – the Keeper of Peace. His eyes can see into your soul and weigh you in a moment.
7. *Ariel* – the Brother of Beasts.

All have large black feathery wings they can kill with and the ability to use light both as a weapon and as a healing power. They also have a demonic form – different to each of them, but no one ever lives after seeing them.

Like all hybrids, they are infertile.

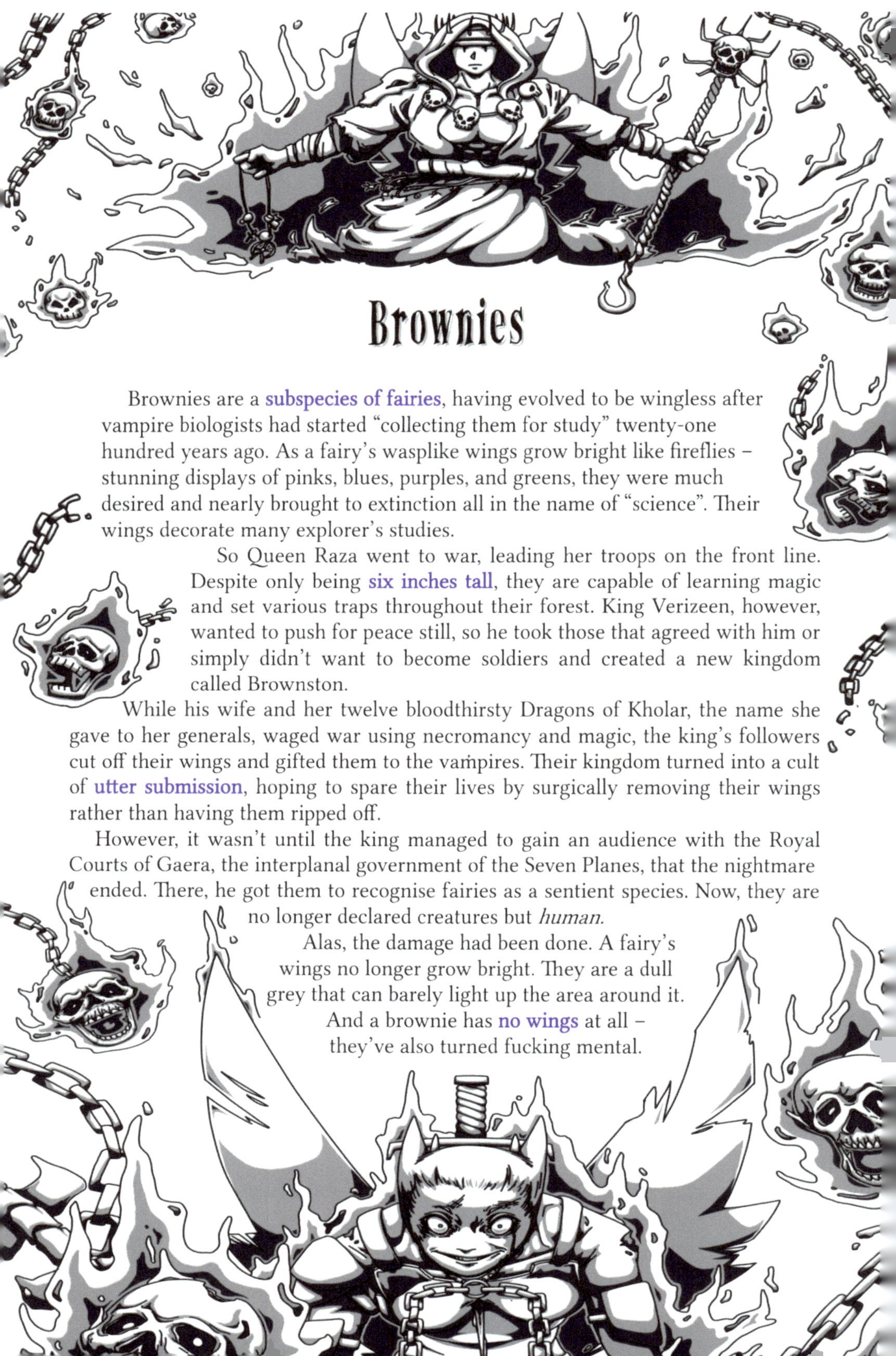

Brownies

Brownies are a subspecies of fairies, having evolved to be wingless after vampire biologists had started "collecting them for study" twenty-one hundred years ago. As a fairy's wasplike wings grow bright like fireflies – stunning displays of pinks, blues, purples, and greens, they were much desired and nearly brought to extinction all in the name of "science". Their wings decorate many explorer's studies.

So Queen Raza went to war, leading her troops on the front line. Despite only being six inches tall, they are capable of learning magic and set various traps throughout their forest. King Verizeen, however, wanted to push for peace still, so he took those that agreed with him or simply didn't want to become soldiers and created a new kingdom called Brownston.

While his wife and her twelve bloodthirsty Dragons of Kholar, the name she gave to her generals, waged war using necromancy and magic, the king's followers cut off their wings and gifted them to the vampires. Their kingdom turned into a cult of utter submission, hoping to spare their lives by surgically removing their wings rather than having them ripped off.

However, it wasn't until the king managed to gain an audience with the Royal Courts of Gaera, the interplanal government of the Seven Planes, that the nightmare ended. There, he got them to recognise fairies as a sentient species. Now, they are no longer declared creatures but *human.*

Alas, the damage had been done. A fairy's wings no longer grow bright. They are a dull grey that can barely light up the area around it. And a brownie has no wings at all – they've also turned fucking mental.

Their submission led to them developing a law where it was illegal to say no. That spiralled into them turning into an overly polite cult, which turned into a 'happiness' cult, which, of course, turned into a sex cult with free use all around.

It's now illegal to be sad or rude or anything other than happy or horny. They have three-hundred-and-eighty-three rules they follow, all listed in a book called *A Good Brownie Does*, and not one of them is normal.

A GOOD BROWNIE:

 ❧ **Invites everyone to an orgy.** Every bug, creature, monster, and human across the Seven Planes must be invited to every orgy hosted (and they host a lot of them). All the souls in the three Underworlds should be invited too. [Inviters never return home because the worlds are fucking vast, and they are little. Marrabelle is an inviter].

 ❧ **Is never sad.** Even if they just found out via an ad in the newspaper that their fiance is dumping them three days before their wedding in order to marry their mother.

 ❧ **Accepts every present they're given with grace.** Even if said present is a killer wasp with an anger problem, given to them by their ex-fiance, who is now their new fiance's maid of honour.

 ❧ **Never cuts in line.** Even if a killer wasp is on the loose and one sting from it is enough to kill a brownie in an instant, and everyone wants to get inside.

 ❧ **Always holds the door open for another.** Regardless of how far away said person is. And regardless of whether the line is a hundred brownies long because everyone's trying to escape a pissed-off wasp. Door holders rarely survive events like this.

 ❧ **Cannot hold someone against their will.** Not even in jail.

 ❧ **Must accept going to jail if they're asked.**

 ❧ **Always relieves someone of pain.** So if they can't heal you, they will kill you as there's no pain in death – they assume everyone will end up in the good part of the underworlds.

 ❧ **Never starts a war.** Even if they get black-out drunk at her ex's wedding.

 ❧ **Never says no.** Even if a serial killer asks to kill her.

Fairies were born from the dying soul of the primordial air elemental after she was killed during the Great Extinction.

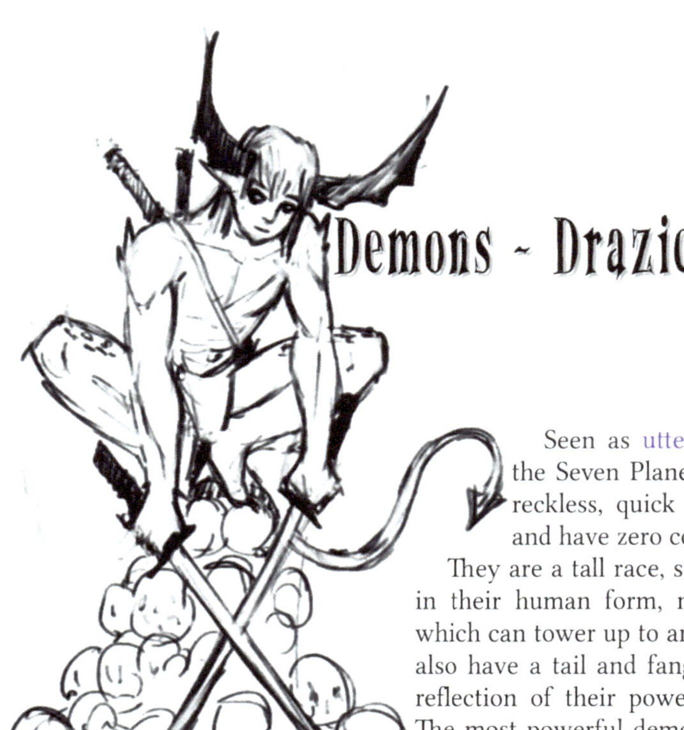

Demons ~ Drazic

Seen as utterly lawless by the rest of the Seven Planes, drazics are brash, loud, reckless, quick to fight, super flirtatious, and have zero control of their impulses.

They are a tall race, standing at six to eight feet in their human form, not including their horns, which can tower up to another twelve inches. They also have a tail and fangs, and their red skin is a reflection of their power, darkening as they age. The most powerful demons have skin so dark red, it almost looks black.

When they shift into their fighting form, they're fifteen to eighteen feet tall.

One of their favourite things to do, other than fighting and fucking, is to discover eknor demon names and then summon them for the dumbest shit. They pass these names around like bongs, so once an eknor demon's name is known by the drazics, their life is basically fucked. Forever.

Despite most races seeing drazics as 'reckless frat boys', however, they actually have a very strong sense of honour, and they are the first to take in stray humans – granted, they take them in as slaves, but their slave-master relationship is nothing like the one on Earth.

As their culture revolves around strength, there is no such thing as rape or assault unless it is done in an un-honourable way (sneak attacks, poison, drugs, telepathy, etc). Both men and women use violence as foreplay. The most desired bachelor or bachelorette (sexism does not exist here; only strong vs weak) is the one who can force a person into submission – so actual fighting with lots of bleeding and bruises is a type of genuine foreplay for them. And this is why they love war. They are basically edging themselves all the time.

Slavery is also rampant in drazic kingdoms, but being a slave is a desired position for a lot of the weaker races as they are then only ever beaten by their masters. To disrespect another's slave is to disrespect them, and that's a recipe for war. It is a master's duty to train their slaves up well enough that they can actually fight their way to freedom. Due to this, the most respected demon is the one with the most self-freeing slaves.

Drazic kingdoms are ruled by either a king, queen, or raan (gender neutral) and their ruling family, which are called highborns. The largest kingdom is ruled by the

Heldrons. These are the guardians to the backdoor of Niflhel, and they are tasked with stopping any souls from escaping from the Norse afterlife, called Hel or Niflhel. They are also the creators of helfire, a whisky that is made with the actual flames of Hel, which is why it will absolutely kill you.

Despite the misnomer, any drazic can become a highborn. All they have to do is kill a highborn and take their place within the family. While they're attempting this, they are called admirers, and it's a bragging right to have a large number of them trying to kill you. Drazics *love* bragging.

They also love betting, gambling, fighting, fucking, and all the other vices. If it hits a dopamine streak, they want it. The black market is just called a market here.

Due to this, the Underground attracts all sorts of criminals and convicts running from the Elv've'Nor (the big daddy branch of the SCU). They are welcomed with open arms as murder, rape, and most of the other crimes aren't crimes here, but kids are *fiercely* protected – which surprises outsiders given their children are all covered in scars, and love is expressed through violence that other cultures would claim is abuse (they rough house and beat, but they do not traumatize), but if anyone fails to protect a child, that child's parents aren't just punished. The entire community is.

They will then be hunted down by the highborns and slaughtered where they are. These hunts are illegal according to the interplanal government, but they have long since decided that as long as drazics do it on the down-low and at least pretend to listen to their rules, they'll turn a blind eye. Because no one wants the drazics as an enemies. Best to leave them to raid the surface of their own world than goad them into attacking the others.

Because they like to raid. A *lot.*

Raiding is a public pasttime and a rite of passage. As the drazic kingdoms expand deep below the Earth, most of the raids throughout the year are only done by the drazics living in the upper Underground cities. However, there are drazic festivals where the highlight is raiding the surface, and practically every demon goes up to have fun for multiple days.

As they're not big on killing weaklings for the sake of it (no sport), rather than killing the surfers on these raids, they fuck them and then force them to fight, dance, sing, drink until they pass out, and otherwise be "merry". They sometimes then take a patch of skin or an ear/finger/other small item off them as a souvenir before heading back down into the Underground.

Payment for the surfers on these days is 100 times what it normally is. Some people only work on the holidays.

Demons ~ Eknor

Eknor demons and drazic demons actually aren't related at all.

The term 'demon' simply comes from the Hevanic (angelic) word for 'disgrace', which stuck after the two kingdoms were ripped apart by the gods and their old feud began anew.

The only thing the two demons (translated: disgraceful races) have in common is that they both live in the Underground of Halzaja. 'Demon' was just a term used by the angels because they're egotistical assholes, but by the time the witches arrived, everyone assumed that 'demon' was a type of race, which was then subdivided into eknor and drazic because drazics aren't big on history or boring facts and eknors are trying to hide their true identity.

You see, not only are eknor demons not demons, but they are actually angels who've fallen from grace – something no one knows.

Once an angel starts to fall, their wings turn putrid and sickly. Then they start to fall off feather by feather. Once they are completely bare, the wings themselves will rot off, and the angel will enter a sort of stasis. A cocoon will develop around them, and it might take weeks before they hatch, but once they do, they will come out as an eknor demon, their type determined by what caused them to fall.

This happens because long ago, the angels made a deal with a djinni. In exchange for the power to emit a light from their palms that can burn the soul of a drazic, they cannot ever lie or commit one of the seven deadly sins. If they do, they'll slowly start to rot, becoming the very thing that they think they are so much better than. An eknor can still burn the soul of a drazic, but as it would give away their shameful secret, they never use that power.

However, a side effect of this deal was the creation of the Deusychosis Plague, a disease that gives its host godlike power for one week, allowing them to bend reality itself. They then die an agonizing death. This disease only affects persepics – the umbrella term for telepaths, telekinetics, and astralists.

And gods.

Due to just how dangerous an outbreak of this plague can be to the balance of the Seven Planes, all fallen angels are hunted down by an archangel. If they come out of their cocoon with no symptoms of the Deusychosis Plague, they will be allowed to live. However, they will be given a name by the archangel, which will allow them to be summoned. This is so the archangels can keep an eye on any developing symptoms without having to chase them down. Any kids they have must also have their names registered with the archangels.

They are often seen in their 'monster' form rather than their human form when summoned, but in the Underground of Halzaja, they use their human form. This is due to drazic demons seeing their 'monster' form as a challenge that they are all too happy to fight.

Eknors are second-class citizens in the Underground, ranking even below a drazic slave. They're seen as 'weak' and pathetic. However, they do have a kingdom that they rule, called Sin. They are not allowed to declare a king though, so they are ruled by seven princes, one from each type of subclass. The drazics are content to let them 'play' with their little plot of land as long as they don't step out of line.

SEVEN PRINCES OF SIN:

- **Vayne, Prince of of Pride** – His family claims to have had a ruling seat since Sin's creation. No one remembers if this is true or not. A born eknor.
- **Rath, Prince of Rage** – Rival to Vayne. A born eknor.
- **Zade, Prince of Lust** – The oldest prince. A silver fox who is into a lot of kinky shit. A fallen angel.
- **Kraven, Prince of Greed** – A street rat (lowest rank) who's recently clawed his way to the top. He was bullied by Vayne and Rath as a kid. A born eknor.
- **Gruj, Prince of Envy** – Misery loves company. A fallen angel.
- **Ryze, Prince of Gluttony** – His kind's bite can infect a person with poison. Inky black sludge will replace the blood of their victim, killing them in two weeks. Not even a healer can save them. A born eknor.
- **Bastian, Prince of Sloth** – Apathetic to everything and a nihilist. Massive black cat energy. A born eknor.

Keres

Walking the outer planes of Purgatory, the keres search for souls who have been brutally murdered on their path of vengeance. They are one of the stronger reapers of the dead as none of the souls they harvest ever wish to go.

Their wings are made of smoke, as are their clothes, and you can often catch glimpses of their body beneath. They are usually covered in blood due to the bodies they visit being pretty badly wounded. The weapons they use to collect souls glow various shades of green, and the heads of said souls can be seen trying to escape.

After collection, a keres figures out which of the three underworlds their soul wishes to go to. They then ferry them to it. This can take years to decades though as going back and forth for one soul isn't very efficient, and what are the souls going to do if they're dragged around for years? Complain to HR?

However, there have been some rumours of keres getting attached to their souls and keeping them like puppets forever…

It is unknown how many souls they can house in a single weapon – though they don't actually have to use a weapon. Some of them carry around great big teddy bears to "be more soothing". This does not work as a calming tactic.

As the outer planes of Purgatory are not connected to the world of the living, in order to reap a oul a keres has to merge the two together. They do this by walking on the ground and sending their innate magic out through their feet, the soles of which are covered in runic tattoos that help them bend the worlds to their will.

When they take a step, the plane of Purgatory that they're in ripples out from their foot like a pebble has been dropped in a lake. The outer planes of Purgatory looks the same as the world of the living, so the dying soul does not often notice that they've passed on – not until they see a reaper of death coming for them.

However, as otherworldly as they may seem, they are still humans, created during the Panhellenic Games by Hel, Hades, and Arawn. They're just doing their jobs and often have working and non-working hours, though it's against most companies' polices to leave half-way through a reaping as this can fuck up the soul and give them a chance to run back to the world of the living. If this happens, every keres around will hunt the soul down, which is why ghosts are non-existent.

Keres do get paid for every soul they collect as well. There's even an illegal and highly unethical service of sending souls to the wrong otherworld in order to collect payment from the gods – or rather their seedy managers. You see, Hades doesn't want anymore souls crowding up his place. Hel wants to piss Hades off because it's fucking hilarious. And Arawn just doesn't want to be left out.

Vampires

The first vampire was called Lilith, and she was created by the gods Dionysus and Hades, who were dating at the time. They gave her the ability to phase so she could get to a witch before they could cast a spell, appear on an angel's back to rip off their wings, or move too fast for a drazic to grab. She drank blood, an ample resource in the Panhellenic Games, to revive herself as well as give her power-ups depending on what species she drank from. Monster or human, each would give her something unique. Due to this, they were winners of the Games multiple times in a row; then they got nerfed (ie: their power-ups are nowhere near as strong as they used to be) and the rules about creating champions were changed because of them.

Witches taste like wine and give them a slight buzz; their blood increases their resistance to magical attacks. Some vampires are sensitive enough that the different types of witches will give them different effects. A necromancer will help them survive more deadly wounds; they taste more like a dry white. A healer is a dark-fruit red and will enhance their senses. A shapeshifter will make them faster and leans more towards a rosé.

Angels taste like a piña colada, and their blood increases a vamp's natural healing ability. Drazics taste like a smokey bourbon and increase their strength. Eknors taste disgusting, like rotten eggs mixed with tar. They make vampires sluggish and slower to heal, so they are rarely drank from.

After Lilith won the Games, the gods created a new world for her and her kind as Halzaja was too inhospitable. They called this place Blódyrió. It was supposed to be a relaxing place full of reading corners (Hades' influence) and party bars (Dionysus'), but the two gods broke up, and Dionysus made it super fucking gloomy "to forever show how much of a buzz kill you are".

In response, Hades simply locked himself up in his library. However, his absence allowed Artemis to take his place, and that bitch is fucking crazy. The Craving and the Blood Moon exists because of her.

As there isn't much light on Blódyrió (never more than the light of dusk or dawn on Earth), the vampires eventually evolved to need less sunlight. They won't burst into flames during daylight though; they're just quick to get sunburnt, and their eyes are more sensitive to the light.

During the Blood Moon, they will be lost to the Craving, their minds reduced to a primitive beast driven only to hunt and fuck. Artemis only wanted them to hunt, but Dionysus added the latter because "hunting isn't fun, Artemis. This is why no one invites you to parties".

Born	Sired
✔ Has blood in their veins and a pulse	✗ No blood or pulse; fuelled by magic
✔ Can phase	✗ Can't phase
✔ When they die, their bodies remain	✗ When they die, they turn to ash
✔ Strong-sun sensitive	✗ Sunlight burns them
✔ Can eat regular food	✗ Can only drink blood*
✔ Fertile	✗ Infertile
✔ Need to cut out their heart or damage both heart and stomach to kill them	✗ Damage to their heart will kill them; no stake required
✔ Can consume 'power-ups' when they drink the blood of angels, demons, or witches	✗ Addicted to their sire's blood as it increases their healing
✔ Can create sired vampires by exchanging their blood	✗ Only zilchers or Earthers can be turned into sired vampires
✔ Much stronger than sired vampires	✗ Heal faster; a severed limb will grow back in a few weeks
	*can eat food but they vomit it back up later

Sometime after the witches migrated from Halzaja to Blódyrió, they used dark magic to bless a vampire with the ability to create sired vampires. Any descendant of this vampire has inherited this ability. Those not of his line can't, but basically every vamp alive today has come from him because it's almost like if you give a person the ability to conquer their corner of the world, they will try.

The reason you need to damage both the heart and stomach of a born vampire in order to kill them is because both of these organs pump blood around their bodies, so as long as one is going, they will have the chance to heal themselves by drinking from another. The reason Varius survived a stab to the heart was due to the curse, but any other vampire would have until the blood in their stomach ran out unless they were able to feed again. Depending on how badly damaged they are, they might constantly need to drink until their heart heals.

The WALL calls born vampires "daywalkers" and sired ones "regs". As they mostly only come across sired vampires, a lot of their information is lacking.

Werewolves

Werewolves were made with the sole purpose of fucking up vampires. After Dionysus refused to let Artemis build Blódyrió just how she wanted it, she decided to make a creature all on her own to kick his champion's ass. It took her multiple Games to create a beast that could do it, but spite is a great motivator for her, and eventually, she came out with the werewolf, which is why their bite and other bodily fluids are poisonous to vampires. A vampire will die within twenty-four hours of being bitten if they can't find a healer or if they don't completely drain a few people to flush the poison from their veins as the bite hinders their own ability to heal.

They stand at seven to nine feet tall in their wolf form. When average to average speed is compared, they are the fastest race. They have a resting heart rate of thirty to forty beats a minute – roughly on par with a human athlete.

Werewolves live in female-dominated packs, with the males often being chased out around their ascension; they travel as lone wolves until they either fight an alpha for his pack or enter another one as a beta.

If a pack grows too large, however, it'll become unstable.

A werewolf isn't born as an alpha, beta, or omega, so they constantly fight for hierarchy. The position of alpha can go unchallenged for decades, but the omega position changes a lot more often than that due to the violent nature of a pack. An omega rarely rises to become a beta, and when they die, their position needs to be refilled.

On Blódyrió, they don't live in large towns or cities because of this.

Their wolf shape is as true to them as their human shape. A werewolf who gives birth while in their wolf shape will give birth to furry young. If they are in their human form, they will give birth to non-furry young. Both are called pups, and they'll shift without control until they hit their ascension.

Forced to partake in the Hunt on Blódyrió any time the moon is either full or red (which can last up for three days and three nights – the moon not always hidden during the day), the creation of Artemis' silver was born.

This is crafted from the goddess' moonlight itself, and it will burn their skin, cause them to spasm uncontrollably, and make them so sick and pale that they look on the verge of death. When a pup undergoes their ascension, they are wrapped in silver chain. Once they can break free, they are deemed "strong enough" to partake in the Hunt. Legends say, during the Blood Moon Hunts, Artemis herself comes down to hunt werewolves and vampires while wearing a red cape. The story of *Little Red Riding Hood* is based on her.

A sun-touched wolf can shift without spasming in agony. This is seen as a curse, but in reality is how Artemis marks who she wants to be her champion for the next Game.

Born	Bitten
✔ Ascension takes place around the age of puberty	✗ Ascension takes place on the first full moon after being bitten
✔ Can control their shift on Earth's full moon	✗ Cannot control their shift on Earth's full moon
✔ Naturally resistant to magic	✗ Magic hurts them like normal
✔ Can bite and change an Earth human	✗ Cannot infect another with their bite
✔ Their shift hurts like hel	✗ Their shift is almost tolerable
✔ Their bite is poisonous to both born and sired vampires	✗ Their bite is only poisonous to sired vampires
✔ Completely clear headed as a wolf	✗ More animalistic as a wolf
✔ Can sire born werewolfs	✗ Cannot sire bitten werewolves

PACK POSITIONS

Alpha – the leaders of the pack; can be male or female, a couple or a poly. They are the only ones who create bitten members. Bitten wolves can be alphas, but they still can't create more bitten members.

Beta – any other member of the pack who isn't an alpha or omega

Omega – the bottom of the pack; often used as a punching bag and attacked in 'pack moral building' sessions. They rarely make it to old age. Every pack has one.

Witches

When the gods went to war with the djinn, they tore them asunder, ripping them into pieces and casting them into the wind. But the djinn's bodies turned into pure magic, leading to violent pockets of energy coursing through the universe. Raging storms, eerie portals to other worlds, and chaos magic developed anywhere a djinni had died, then spread out like a sea of vengeance. So the gods collected all the djinn energy they could – though legends warn of battlefields too deadly or large to clean up, and they put all this magic aside, unsure of what to do with it.

Until one day, the Morrighan (Gaelic Goddess of War and Witchcraft), Hecate (Graecian Goddess of Spells), and Freya (Queen Goddess of the Aesir-Vanir) decided to create a champion for the Panhellenic Games together; when they placed a shard of a djinni's soul into it, the first witch was born.

They were victorious in the arena, and then they were placed on Halzaja. Given they couldn't fly, they were sent below to live with the drazics. It is from them that they learned how to summon eknor demons, and that is why all of their ancient text is written in Drazic. However, after the creation of Blódyrió, the majority of them migrated to the new world. Because of this, they do not have an issue with sunlight.

Most sups will live until they are killed, but witches are one of the ones who will not. Due to the violent magic in their veins, it limits their lifespan to around two hundred years. The three goddesses did not fix this as they wanted this limitation on them as they feared what would happen if they lived long enough to learn enough spells to take on the gods.

Due to being born with magic in their blood, witches can use pre-made wands before their ascension. However, they cannot control their own magic until they hit their ascension. At that point though, most prefer to use tattoos to control their magic as it's far too easy to misplace a wand – or get it knocked out of their hand in a fight. This is why, although custom wands are a lot more powerful than the tattoos, they are basically only used by witches in training.

Every witch has an innate ability that they are born with, and this develops during their ascension. This has lead to different "types" of witches.

A FEW TYPES OF WITCHES

🌿 **Healer** – they're able to manipulate and enhance the body's ability to heal itself. Their healing potions are stronger than average as well. Once a person is healed with magic, however, it is practically permanent. Most healers use their power for good, thankfully, but dark healers make amazing torturers. They can also kill with a single touch, using their magic in "reverse".

🌿 **Electric** – can control electricity, from large bolts of lightning to small pulses through their victim's brain, effectively controlling them by hijacking their nervous system. They can also use this ability to specialise in electronic magic, controlling and hacking electronics with relative ease.

🌿 **Shielders** – can create bubbles and walls that stop everything – magic, air, people, etc. from going through them. The stronger a witch, the harder it is for someone to break through their shield.

🌿 **Shapeshifters** – can change their entire appearance and atomic make-up to match any creature, monster, or human that they have had time to study. This can take anywhere to a few minutes for a face to an hour for the full body or weeks to months to years for a full atomic make-up (depending on how often they see each other – they can study over time; they don't have to be with them 24/7). However, they can't replicate powers they don't have, copy their dialect, move like they do, or have any of their memories. All those things need to be learned. The stronger ones can mimic non-biological items on the outside, but inside they are still made of flesh and blood.

🌿 **Soul Magic Users** – can develop in a variety of ways from creating weapons that are crafted from their soul (these deal a lot of damage, even to those with an innate resistance to magic, like werewolves), to using soul dolls, which allow them to control, spy on, and even kill their subject from afar. Khalid will later use this to make his *kira* orgasm while he's away from her.

🌿 **Telekinetics** – can affect both living and non-living things without having to touch them. The latter are a lot easier to control as living creatures can fight them and their bodies are constantly changing. A strong one like Caden can rip a person apart at their atoms.

THE MAGIC
SYSTEM

There are two types of magic: dormant magic and magic. (The real distinction is god-touched magic and djinn-soul magic respectively, but no one knows that.)

Dormant magic is any magic that runs through the veins of any human that isn't a witch. This is what allows werewolves to shift at will, vampires to phase, mermaids to walk on land, etc. Dormant magic is tied to the body and is triggered during one's ascension – a magical puberty that usually takes place at the same time as one's biological puberty but not always.

Then there is *magic*.

This exists only in witches (fairies are created from the soul of a dead primordial, which is unknowingly a type of djinn, but not all of them have magic, so those that do are still called 'witches' even though they are technically just fairies with magic). This magic can be controlled to affect things outside of their body by casting spells and is further divided into: innate magic and learned magic. Innate magic is the magic a witch is born with. It doesn't manifest until their ascension. Learned magic is anything a witch can learn to do outside of their innate ability. They can use such magic through a wand before their ascension, but they are not able to control it very well. Learned magic is often colour based: red for attack or aggressive magic, blue for defensive or calmer magic, and green for otherworldly connects like necromancy.

To use magic, one first needs a conduit in order to control it. Witches who have just passed their ascension often use a custom wand for this, though the weaker ones can get away with using a premade (a wand made in mass production). Despite wands being the strongest conduits out there, they are often lost, forgotten, or stolen. For this reason, most witches learn to use their hands as conduits, and they place runic tattoos on their body as shortcuts for their more common spells. One's voice can also be used as a conduit, but this is extremely difficult to master and often ends in death or permanent disfigurement during the training stage, so it's very rare for a witch to do.

All magic causes a backwash of energy on the user. If the user is too weak or exhausted, that energy can seriously hurt them or even kill them from the inside out, starting with consuming their organs and bones. Any damage taken this way is resistant to any healing magic and takes a while to recover from.

All magic requires sacrifice, and agreeing to give up your kidney in exchange for using magic while you're exhausted and then trying to sneak around that by healing yourself after is a recipe for death. Magic (djinn) doesn't like being tricked.

If too much magic is swirling around inside someone – whether they're a witch or not, they run the risk of developing loka, a type of magical disease that affects the blood and causes massive organ failure. Monsters, creatures, Earthers, and zilchers – due to the low level of magic inside them– can usually be healed from it entirely. The magic simply needs time to flush itself out of its system, so as long as a healer or normal doctor can keep up with the constant damage, they will recover as soon as all the magic is out.

With all other humans, there is no cure for loka, only management. Werewolves, vampires, shifters, etc can all live a long and healthy life as long as they don't use their dormant magic. Every time an infected vampire phases or a shifter changes between their forms, however, they will shorten their lifespan. If a werewolf is forced to shift under Artemis' moons, their disease will progress rapidly due to the Craving.

In witches, however, magic is ingrained with every part of them, so they will only have three or four months to live after developing the disease. Due to this, they're extremely careful about how much magic they use at all times. If too much magic starts to build up in their blood stream, they must not use any spells until it's back down to a "safe" level. This could take months to a year or more. However, they will never get their base level back down to what it was, so the more often they use a large amount of magic at once, the higher their chances are of developing loka.

Outside of the normal rules of magic, you have three more types: chaos, dark, and curses. Chaos magic develops when magic is corrupted. This is what happened to the djinn when the gods killed them, leading to highly unstable pockets of energy. And when Sau was hit with a violent spell while pregnant with Rudy, he was born with chaos magic. This is why his power seeps from his skin and is constantly trying to explode. It requires a battle of wills 24/7. Ascensions start well before puberty.

Dark magic is extremely easy to use (though not control), but requires a larger blood sacrifice than the spell's benefit. Many cases of people vanishing into thin air, such as the Roanoke settlers and the Lost Army of Cambyses can be traced back to this. Sacrifices can be taken from anywhere in the world. They do not have to be beside the witch when the spell is cast, but if they are not, then the witch does not get to choose who is sacrificed. Sometimes, it is their loved ones – the very people they are trying to protect.

Curses are one of the easiest types of magic to cast as djinn are easily tempted to fuck people up. However, there must always be a way to break the curse, and it is up to the caster to decide what it is. The stronger the curse, the more ridiculously easy the curse has to be to break, but it is up to the cursed to figure out what random thing the caster picked, which can be difficult. Not wanting to take any chances, Sau worked around this when she cursed Varius by coupling it with dark magic.

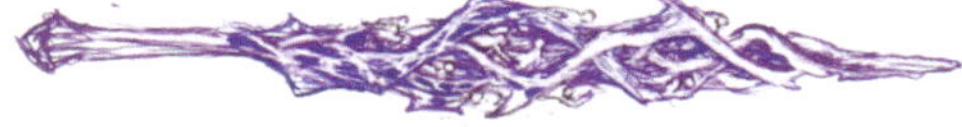

If a human is born with a lot of magic (dormant or otherwise), when they hit their ascension, they will start to pulse. Their magic will rip free uncontrollably at random intervals. The stronger the magic, the longer and more dangerous these pulsing sessions can be. Rudy pulsed for years before he learned to control it. Sau pulsed inside of her coma for around eight months.

Blood Bonds

This is a spell only witches can cast due to an ancient deal one made with a djinni long ago. They can bind themselves to either another witch or a non-witch, but all the witches involved have to make a payment, which has to be something that'll tear the couple apart because djinn find this funny. So for someone who is over-the-top jealous, they might have to allow all of their brothers to fuck their girl. Or to let her get aroused by watching one of their brothers fuck someone else. The payment is unique to each person and is up to the witch to decide. However, if the payment is not harsh enough, then the blood bond will be rejected, and the person who started the blood bond will die unless they kill the other person first.

To start the blood bond, a witch simply needs to wish for it hard enough as it's an emotionally-charged spell, then exchange blood with the person they wish to be bonded to. To end it, the payment(s) must be made and sealed with sex magic, which requires the person who didn't start it to be denied an orgasm three times. The blood bond rune is then drawn onto their body with bodily fluids, and the final round of blood is shared. These steps can be done at any time, with any length of time in between as long as they continuously share blood.

If a non-witch is part of the deal, the blood must be exchanged relatively slowly. A witch needs a certain amount of magic in their system to survive, so replacing their blood with non-witch/magic blood too much, too fast will kill them.

Once a blood bond is started, it must be fed. Otherwise, it will take the blood/life of the person who started it as payment. You cannot end a blood bond once it has begun. It will gradually consume the amount of blood shared, and this process can be quickened if either party uses the gifts they get from it, which includes being able to feel their partner's location and emotions, as well as push their own emotions down the bond to them. When used excessively, this can lead to it becoming almost impossible to discern which emotions are yours and which are theirs, which is why Kiyana fell for Khalid so fast – her emotions were being influenced by his. You can erect a temporary wall to stop this by simply wanting it hard enough.

Blood bonds are not just for life, but for all your lives. You will reincarnate close enough together to have a good chance of meeting again and again and again. However, as with all reincarnations, you do not retain your previous memories. You will be pulled to each other by a "sixth sense" sort of deal. You randomly quit your job to apply to an ad you saw; you walk a new way home from work, etc.

Most couples who blood bond, however, turn into archnemeses within a year due to the harsh payment. This festers into a hate that magically affects the blood bond.

Healing

The speed and quality of one's innate healing varies from race to race and from human to human, but it doesn't activate until one's ascension. Due to this, any scars you see on a human (minus an Earther or zilcher) were most likely received when they were kids.

Additionally, werewolves, shifters, and shapeshifters can heal themselves through shifting, but a shifter (a human who can only shift into a single animal, such as a wolf or an aranthae) can only heal minor wounds this way. This is because both of their forms are their real forms and injuries transfer between their bodies. The shift increases the healing magic in their veins, and this is what allows them to fix minor injuries.

A werewolf, however, can heal all minor wounds and some middle-ranged ones with a single shift due to the vast flood of magic through their system. As their shift is more violent than a shifter's (who shifts flawlessly and without pain), they require a higher amount of healing magic in order to repair all the damage wrought by their change. This influx has the additional effect of allowing them to heal from all but major wounds. Which is a pretty amazing skill to have, especially in the Panhellenic Games, but nothing matches the self-healing power of a shapeshifter.

Shapeshifters can heal from anything that doesn't kill them immediately as long as they reduce enough mass as to be whole again despite their injury. For instance, a shapeshifter cut in half can heal fully if he shifts into a bunny as they have true mastery over their body, and anytime they downsize, they remove mass anyway. They can also turn an arm with a hole in it into a leg, or a stomach into a tentacle, etc. Stronger shapeshifters can shift into their normal form when they're already in their normal form as a way to move their fatal injuries to somewhere less serious. This can occur in the blink of an eye, making them a deadly opponent who doesn't fucking die.

The only thing none of these races can heal from is any damage inflicted *during the change*. For shifters and werewolves, their innate healing ability is faster while in their beast forms.

Vampires are another human that can increase their innate healing ability, but they do it by consuming blood. The blood of a regular human or a vampire who has not yet sired only increases the healing affect a little. If the blood is that of a sire, it will allow them to heal even faster and from more serious wounds. If that sire is also their sire (meaning they were sired by them), then that healing power is increased again. However, the most potent blood is that of a bookworm thanks to Hades' sense of humour when he and Dionysus made the first vampire. The more books one has read, the more powerful their blood is to a vampire. If they are currently suffering from a book hangover, watch the fuck out, because that vampire is getting a damn strong boost.

The fact that Lilith, the first vampire, drank from Hades and he *liked* it is what caused him and Dionysus to break up.

A witch with the innate power to heal does not heal any faster than other witches unless they use their magic to heal themselves. An angel's innate healing is severely affected if they're falling, especially where it concerns their wings. A drazic demon's innate healing is the strongest, and those over a thousand years old can even come back from having been blown to smithereens. As they were created by the Three Furies, they have a type of "nine lives" deal, but they only get one extra life per thousand years, and it caps at three. Earthers and zilchers have pretty slow innate healing abilities.

However, if one receives a wound from a cursed tool that affects the healing ability, no shifting, blood, or extra "life" will heal it.

And any wounds healed by magic – whether via potion, wand, or direct, will be a permanent fix as soon as the magic has time to set. This is why Varius lost a bit of his sight when he used potions to fix his eyes and wasn't able to get to a proper healer in time to reverse the effects. Healing potions are only for minor injuries or for use in the field as they are off-the-shelf spells, and given every body and injury is unique, they don't always fix things correctly. They'll heal the more serious wounds first, but one potion is rarely enough to heal major injuries. They are deliberately created to have a long set time so that the taker can get to a proper healer and have them reverse any negative effects of the potion in time to heal them correctly.

Healers can learn to cut open magically healed wounds in order to re-heal them,

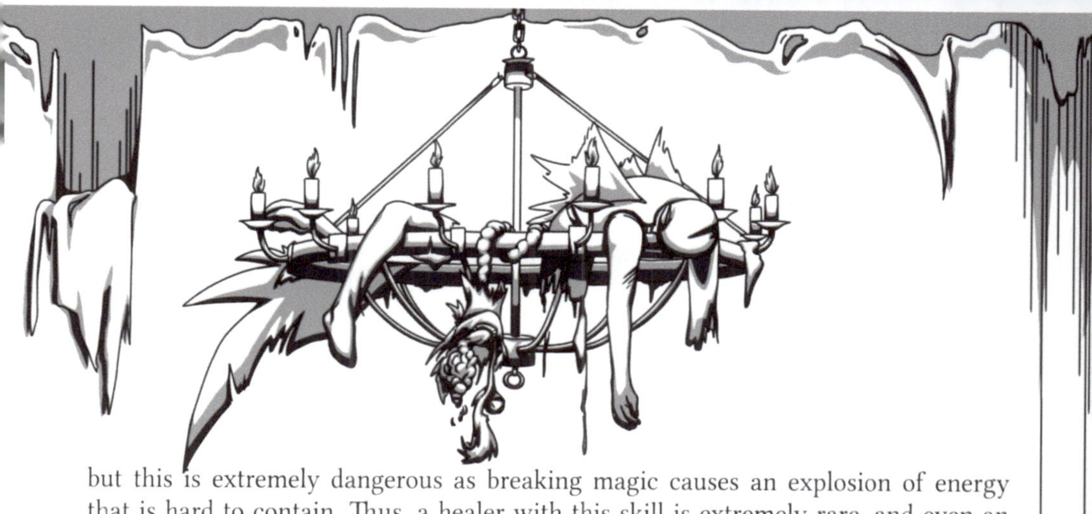

but this is extremely dangerous as breaking magic causes an explosion of energy that is hard to contain. Thus, a healer with this skill is extremely rare, and even an experienced one can very easily do a lot more damage than good. Breaking magic is a rejection of a god's blessing, and they do not take such things kindly. Any witch who is practicing this type of magic must be vetted and licensed by the Royal Courts of the Seven Planes (RCSP), an interplanal government that was created after the Great Extinction in an attempt to stop any future Great Wars. With how dangerous magic can be, the Royal Courts often oversee its development.

Necromancy

Anyone can learn necromancy, but it takes a very stupid/insane person to want to do this as the only way to learn it is by killing yourself over and over again so you can step into the planes of Purgatory.

Not everyone can be bought back though because necromancers return one's soul to their body. They're not Doctor Frankenstein. They're not even good healers as healing works with the body. Necromancy is more blunt force, and if it's used on a person who's alive, it makes them explode. So you need a healer to repair any heart or brain damage, reattach any severed parts, and stop the body from decaying while you head off into Purgatory to grab the soul you want, which can sometimes take a while.

If you attempt to put someone back into their body when it is no longer capable of holding them, there is a chance that a large part of their soul ends up inside you. This hurts like a bitch, and only one of you will survive. You're normally the winner because their body is already divided into two, so you have the advantage, but it's not something you want to ever try. Especially since to resurrect someone, you have to give up a bit of your soul in order to enter the planes of Purgatory. This cost must be paid regardless of whether you're successful at finding and bringing back the person you want or not. It's not a big slice of your soul – nowhere near enough to be dangerous, but it is still a very finite and highly prized resource, which is why raisers of the dead charge two arms and three legs.

This starting risk is only increased when you actually get to Purgatory. The planes do not take kindly to living souls (with the exception of keres, who, over millennia, have evolved to be in harmony with it). There aren't as many monsters there to kill you like on the Plane of Monsters, but the world itself sucks away at your soul, turning you mad step by step.   .

On their first trip (ie: their teacher kills them), students can only stay there for a second. This tolerance is built up over time – a *lot* of time. The average student studies for thirty to forty years – if they survive that long.

Because it's not just the world itself and the monsters that attack you. The reapers want to beat the shit out of you or drag you down to the underworlds for messing with the 'natural' order. But the most danger comes from the souls that are wandering the planes. They're drawn not to your soul as you wander around but to the body you left back in the world of the living. The body that is acting as a tether between the worlds.

Now, they can't actually step into your body and take it as theirs because one's body is entwined to their soul. But that doesn't stop them from trying, and every time they do, your body takes damage. If they destroy it before you can get back or if they just destroy the tether or if a reaper decides to push the worlds back apart, then you're stuck in Purgatory forever. Not dead. Not alive. Never able to be resurrected. Some say this is how the first keres was born...

The ridiculous risk combined with the decades of training required makes necromancy one of the rarest forms of magic to practice. However, you do get a cool eye out of it – one turns a vivid, almost luminescent green and gives you the ability to see the planes of Purgatory while you're still in the world of the living. You also get paid whatever you want to charge, which leads to most necromancers being selfish, egotistical pricks.

When a soul is resurrected, a vast amount of power is required. You have to open a portal to Purgatory, heal part of the body, and reattach the soul. That influx of energy lingers in your 'patient' long after they've returned, making them nearly immortal. For the next few hours, they will auto-revive and heal from every injury within seconds. The only way to kill them is by removing both their head and heart, which is nowhere near as easy as it normally is.

It is entirely inhumane and illegal on every one of the Seven Planes, but there are whispers of people having taken advantage of this. Varius heard about a kingdom called Raza that had an elite group of soldiers. These women and men (they are a matriarchal society) would be murdered, then resurrected right before their mission, making them an unstoppable force. However, due to all the different bits of souls inside them, they will eventually either die or go mad.

Born necromancers are able to use older and more damaged bodies without need of a healer. However, they have the added risk of being targeted by body part traffickers. A single finger of one went for three thousand dollars in 1947, a head for sixty thousand, and their special eye for a hundred and twenty-five.

Potions

Potions are **emotionally charged**. The stronger the emotion pushed into it during its creation, the more effective it is. The ingredients used to create it are important as well, but you can follow the recipe exactly and still get a subpar potion if you don't inject the feeling. Happiness and laughter for healing potions. Anger and aggression for combat potions, etc. For this reason, a lot of incubi and succubi get into potion making as a career. There are rumours, however, of the first empath having just been found somewhere on Gaera…

Death rune

Silence rune

Runes

Blood Bond rune

Runes are any shapes imbued with magic. However, the shape itself can affect the magic it holds, which is why there are **common runes**. For instance, the silence rune often looks like a mouth that's stitched shut. A scry rune – an eye within a circle. Anything to do with magic, often includes flames or wavy, pointy shapes. But the strongest runes are those that are uniquely designed by the witch as those are made **"with soul"**.

Runes help control and strengthen the power of spells as they act as conduits and batteries. This is why they are tattooed on the skin of witches. When used, they glow either **red** (violence, aggression, power, etc), **blue** (protection, defence, peace, etc), or **green** (other world, spirits, soul, mind, etc). If broken (which doesn't happen when the skin is cut or rubbed off due to the magic being connected to the body as a whole), then an explosion of energy will occur.

A rune will lose magic over time and must be topped up. When they are tattooed by the witch, on the witch, their lifeforce will do this automatically. If they are tattooed on someone else, the person who created it must manually charge them up every so often, such as when Dayne and Micha gave each other tracking tattoos. Micha gave Dayne one that she claims was a bunny, but it 100% just looks like a dick with eyeballs and ball hair "for whiskers" and shooting sperm "for ears". Dayne gave her a crooked smiley face with a straight-up dick for a nose.

Soul Magic

Soul magic affects the soul itself, which is why not even werewolves have a resistance to it. Most users learn how to craft soul dolls out of alexandrite, which is a very rare stone throughout all of the Seven Planes. A lot of people think that soul magic is an instant kill you can't train against, but in truth, to use soul magic, you have to put a bit of your own soul on the line. If the person you're targetting is stronger than you, they can kill you when you try to use a soul doll of them. Or if you're using a soul whip, and they grab hold of it, they can do damage to the whip itself, which will resonate back to your soul. This is why soul swords are not used.

Once the target of a soul doll is killed, the alexandrite turns black and is no longer usable. However, if the doll is separated from them before death, you can craft another doll from it.

Summoning Circles

Summoning circles only work on eknor demons, but they can be **made by anyone**, regardless of whether they have dormant magic or true magic. Earthers and zilchers can also create them.

There are three main parts to drawing a summoning circle:
1. **Summoning Lock** – two or more circles are drawn slightly spaced apart, with lines connecting them. If there are three circles, the lines form a triangle, with a circle at each point. If there's four, it's a cross. If there's five, it's an envelope. Six, a snowflake. Seven, same as six with the seventh circle in the middle. Etc. The goal is to connect the circles with as many intersections as possible. The more of these lines that touch a circle, the stronger that circle is. The stronger the demon, the bigger the summoning lock.
The purpose of the summoning lock is to summon the attributes you desire, such as: power, obedience, truth, soul, chaos, violence, protection, etc.
2. **Calling** – used to clarify which demon you wish to call forth by writing its name and demon type inside the inner containment circle. The more you repeat their name, the stronger the calling.
3. **Containment Circle** – These are the solid rings that envelope the entire working. You need a minimum of two – an inner ring, which wraps around the summoning lock and calling, and an outer, which circles the inner ring. Each additional ring is also called an outer ring. The **inner ring** is so nothing inside it can escape. The **outer rings** are so nothing outside can break in.
Between each outer ring are runes and workings of power. The strength of these outer rings are then sacrificed to make the inner ring even stronger, but the side effect of this makes the outer rings weak to break. Meaning that if someone was inside the summoning circle, it would be really hard for them to break out, but if someone wanted to break in or break the circle from the outside, a toe scrub would normally do it. Sometimes a hard breath is enough. For this reason, DO NOT, get into a heated argument with a demon and try to attack them or yell in their face. Many people have died by accidentally toeing the line and thus breaking their outer ring, which then breaks the inner ring, which then lets the scary demon out.

For the stronger demons, you could need over a hundred outer rings to sacrifice in order for the inner ring to be strong enough to hold them.

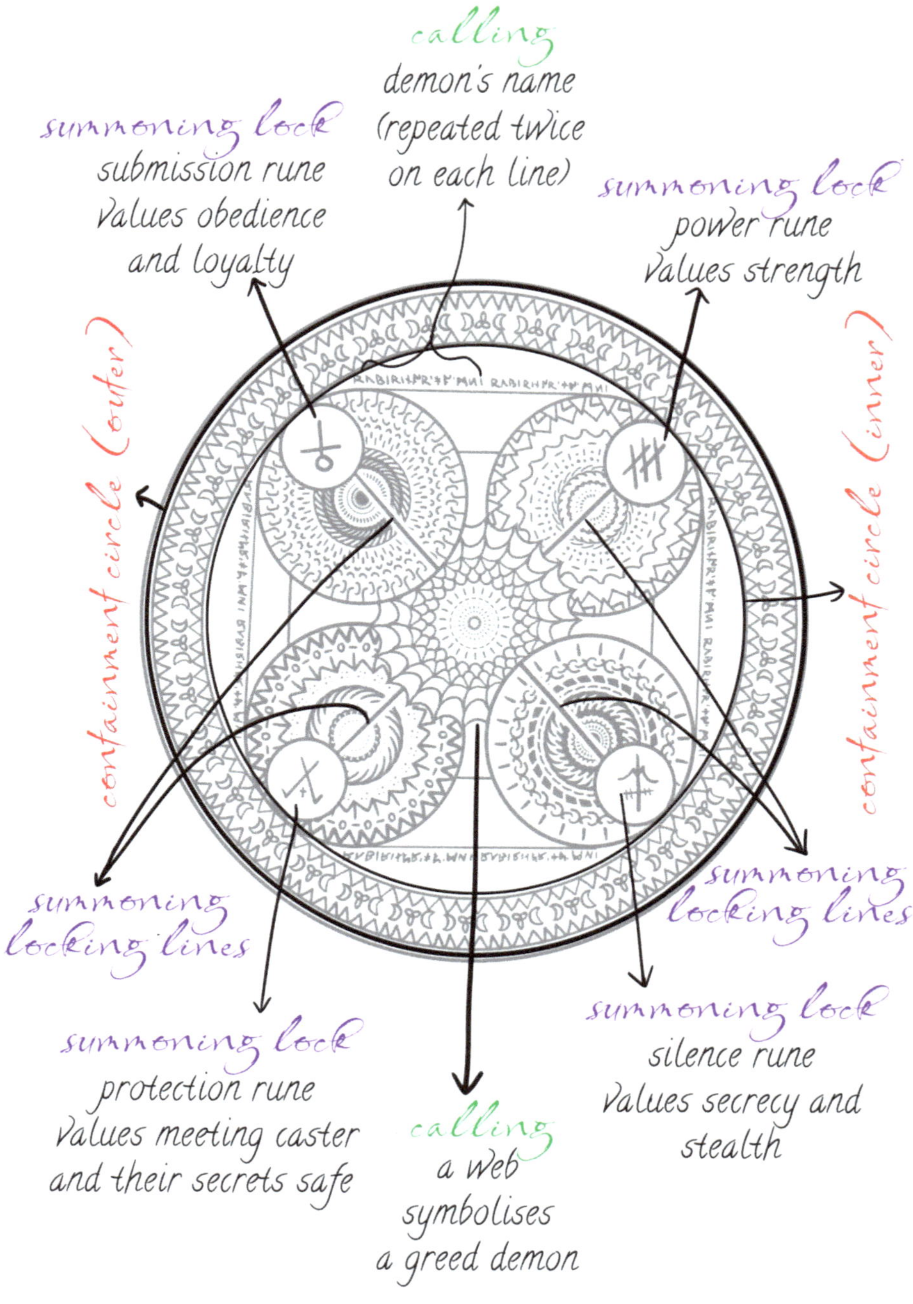
calling
demon's name
(repeated twice
on each line)

summoning lock
submission rune
Values obedience
and loyalty

summoning lock
power rune
Values strength

containment circle (outer)

containment circle (inner)

summoning
locking lines

summoning
locking lines

summoning lock
protection rune
Values meeting caster
and their secrets safe

calling
a web
symbolises
a greed demon

summoning lock
silence rune
Values secrecy and
stealth

You also need to say an incantation to activate the summoning spell and call the demon forth. Most demons only need one to two sentences as they cannot resist the call. Stronger demons can require chanting for a long fucking time.

The incantation sounds cool because it's in Drazic, but it's basically just telling the demon to get their ass over here and what you'll do if they don't. So talk as much smack as you want, but you better be able to back it up, especially if it gets free as the demon will hear all of this when they're being summoned.

If a demon appears and fancy shit starts happening inside the circle like smoke and fire, don't go ooh and awww. That's them testing the strength of your magic. They are about to fuck your shit up.

Only a handful of people throughout history have managed to summon a demon prince. Only two people –Lou Lesli Black and Maddox Snail Shadow– have managed to summon one and live.

Teleportation Circles

Teleportation circles are a pre-defined network of portals that can be accessed by anyone with the "key".

To make them, one first marks out an area, called a domain, with various runes imbued with their magic. A minimum of nine points must be established around the perimeter. The best location for a domain is an open space with barely any human traffic. This lowers the risk of passersby messing with the runes – either on accident or on purpose, and therefore makes it safer to use. Most domains average roughly 900ft^2, but according to legend, there once was a witch called Jocelin Landaverde that created a domain that was twenty-million miles squared – roughly the size of Manhattan, New York.

Once the first domain is established, a second one must be connected to it. This is done by weaving tens of thousands of magical fibres between the two sets of runes. When someone activates the portal, all of these invisible strands will latch onto their body and pull them towards the destination circle.

If these threads snap, it can cause serious injury or even death as the body parts connected to the snapped threads can become lost between the circles. Or worse, those threads will flay together, twisting into a knotted mess and causing the body to also become twisted. There have been an unsettling number of cases where a person has stepped through a portal, only to come out severely disfigured on the other side.

Obviously, this means that any tampering with the circles can have really serious and devastating consequences. This is why they are locked down tight with various levels of security. For those who wish to stop anyone else from using their network of portals, they can easily corrupt a few threads as well if their security measures are triggered. Thus, it's extremely rare for anyone to use another person's teleportation circle.

To connect a third, fourth, fifth, etc, portal to the network, one must increase the number of runes in all of the domains to make sure they aren't being overloaded by the pull of the threads, as well as manually connecting each portal to the others. For this reason, teleportation networks rarely have more than a dozen circles if they're all interlocked. However, it is common for much bigger networks to exist, with each portal only connecting to a few other ones rather than all of them.

Anything within the domain can be teleported. You just need to draw a double-lined black circle, called the teleportation circle, around the items with two of your fingers while pushing your magic into it. This is a lot faster to do than setting up the domain (which can take hours to days), and should only take one to three minutes. But don't rush it. What you are doing is checking the strength of the threads, as well as letting your magic memorise every particle of what you wish to send through so you can unravel any knots or reattach any snapped threads should the worst occur. The more safety you apply here, the more likely things are to reach their destination in one piece. If the circle is broken, DO NOT continue. Erase what remains and start over as it could have caused a magical backlash strong enough to have broken the threads.

Once the circle is connected, chant the incantation to open the doorways. If you are going through them yourself, be prepared for it to hurt like a bitch as all the threads grab on to you and pull at slightly different speeds – not enough to kill you (if they are done correctly) but almost enough to make you wish it did.

All teleporters on Earth must be trained and licensed by the SCU. Their circles must also undergo rigorous testing after every five uses or twenty circles drawn, whichever comes first.

Despite the increased level of safety over the years, teleportation magic is still rarely used as those who wish to travel long distances simply fly or pay someone to phase them. Those methods are much safer.

Wands

The most famous wandmaker currently alive in all of the Seven Planes is Suzanne Ledford. She is a wonderer at heart, and she spends months to years getting to learn about the items she uses within her wands. She's also an extremely powerful witch, and if she wanted to try to take over the Seven Planes, she would have a pretty good run as she is both a necromancer and a soul magic user.

There are two types of wands: premades and customs. Premade wands are those that are mass produced and are mainly used by humans who have dormant magic, although healing wands are used by all. A set number of spells are loaded onto the wand. A max of four different types of spells can be loaded onto one premade. The wand can be used by anyone, and combat wands revolutionized warfare as much as guns did on Earth.

All premades are legally required to be triggered by the word, "Iactus" so that when they are used as evidence in court, the courts can actually prove what spell they do. Black market wands don't use this word.

Custom wands are the most powerful way to cast a spell. They must be tuned to its wielder, and this can take months to years, depending on how powerful the wand is. You can still use the wand during this warm-up phase, but it won't be anywhere near as strong until you're attuned to it. The reasons most witches don't use wands despite their power is: 1. expense, 2. putting it down and forgetting where, 3. doesn't fit in a pocket, 4. can be taken during combat, leaving you defenceless.

The only race that can use wands before their ascension are witches. However, it isn't safe to give a pre-ascension kid a custom wand as they are a lot more powerful, and they aren't restricted to only a few spells.

To make a wand, you get your base material – wood, bone, horns, antlers, metal, rock, etc, anything that's well enough to carve or mould. Then you work it with your magic to portray the power you want, adding other materials to it as you go – the same concept as making a potion. The reason Suzanne Ledford's such a badass wand maker is that she can coax the lingering soul from all the material she uses back into "life". It isn't aware, but it hums with much stronger magic.

Micha's wand was crafted from the antler of a kezja alicorn (Varius called it a horn, but he's wrong; they fall off), which is native to the world of Halzaja – where the demons and angels live. Kezjic (plural) value freedom above all else, and if they end up in captivity, they commit suicide. Depression also leads to a weakening of one's soul. Knowing this, Suzanne is always careful to work in harmony with the creatures and things she uses in her wands.

Wards

The strength of a ward vastly depends on the power of the witch who created it, though multiple witches can combine their magic together to create a more powerful ward, and they can also add power to it over time. Generational wards are one of the strongest – *if* they are fed correctly.

The bigger a ward is, the more magic it requires. One that circles the entirety of the Shadow property, which is thirty acres, would be relatively weak even if a witch as strong as Sau created it. This is why multiple members of the Shadow family add their magic to it.

A ward continuously eats energy – it has a base level, and it spikes every time it is tested, so if it is not fed daily (or more so if it's heavily used), it will eventually consume itself until it dissolves. Wards are rarely broken in the sense of aggressively bypassing the spell and causing it to shatter (Micha did this only because she had magic-eating fire, which helped her to reduce the explosion, and it still hurt like hel). Instead, they are coaxed into eating themselves – either entirely or just enough to bring it down temporarily (think of it as having a nap after a massive dinner, which is what Aleric caused in *Madness Behind the Mask*).

A ward can be as specific as a witch wants and as dangerous. Most wards just stop certain people from entering without killing them because the more lethal a ward is, the more energy it requires to create and the more it eats every time it's used, meaning an enemy can easily overload a touch-and-instantly-die ward by sacrificing a few people to it (*cough cough* Aleric). Having it only hurt people but spit them back out will allow it to last exponentially longer. The power equivalent is roughly one thousand "safe" attempts to one kill. If someone keeps trying to push through after being stopped, however, even if it's a "safe" ward, they will be killed – unless they happen to be stronger than the ward, which is unlikely.

It takes even more energy to hold the person on the ward itself, like a fly in a web, than it does to kill. However, it doesn't take anywhere near as much energy to just tag them so you can hunt them down later.

Wards normally extend up high enough that a human can't jump over them and into the ground enough that they can't dig under them either. However, they rarely have ceilings because the amount of extra energy that requires could be better put to strengthening the walls of the ward as no one other than Aleric is dumb enough to fall from the fucking sky. The exception is if you're warding against angels or other fliers. In which case, geodesic domes are the strongest shape to use, but they are more complicated to create.

Wards are a **shimmering light-blue**, their presence barely susceptible unless you look at it head-on. Therefore, when looking up at a ward to see how high you need to go to jump over it, you can't tell, making such an action highly risky as even a safe ward will kill you if you try to force your way through, and changing direction during a jump is impossible.

Antonio managed to bypass Micha's ward in the Shadow House that first time because she imagined werewolves in their fully shifted form when she created it, and he has the power to partially shift. As wards listen to their *exact* requirements, Micha would've had to imagine every possible combo of a human-werewolf shift in order to keep him out. If she'd made a witch-only ward, she would've been fine, but given she knew they had a witch, that wouldn't have helped her either. The reason Varius is allowed through witch-only wards is because part of him is a witch, and 'access only' wards work on imagining the type of person that can come through. He can also pass through vampire-only wards. If you want the ward to be person specific, you need to feed them that DNA often. The average-sized ward requires more than a litre a day though, so that's not ideal.

Placing a **ward on a person**, such as what Khalid did when he protected his kira from being raped, is extremely dangerous. The constant backwash of magic will kill the host in a relatively short time. Khalid only took this risk because 1. he knew it'd only be for a very short time, 2. he was banking on its mere presence being enough of a deterrent that it wouldn't actually be tested, 3. he needed to do something fast, and 4. he tied it to himself so that it would end as soon as he died, meaning he could easily kill himself to release it before it hurt her if push came to shove. Have you noticed this mother fucker is a bit drastic?

Drazic Language

The Drazic language is more spoken through **body language** than it is through infliction, growls, and words. A bare of the teeth or a raise of the brow or a roll of the eyes can change the meaning of the words *kaz-ij* (kill him) from "Let's kill this fucker now" to "Dammit! We should've killed him when we had the chance, but we can't now because our sister is in love with him. Urgh!" *Kaz-ik* can mean both "Go kill yourself; I hate you" and "You look very tired; as a friend I am telling you to go to sleep."

It's a very complicated language despite the elementary sentence structure and extremely limited word bank. A lot of phrases have **double meanings**. Witches have tried to flesh out the language more, so they use a version of it that is a bit more definitive, but the reason the Drazic language works so well with magic is that it is more freeing and less rigid, which is what magic likes. Magic is fluid; it must be allowed to dance.

BASIC SENTENCE STRUCTURE IN DEMON DRAZIC

Verb-subject (everything else is "said" with gestures, growls, and tone)

Loiek-ij <[relationshipped]-him>
Demon word <literal translation, with the words in [xxx] ones that don't translate>

said aggressively with a baring of the teeth and growls might mean =
our relationship is that of archenemies; I will kill him and eat his bones
or
he ate the last slice of cake; I'm going to beat him, then fuck his brains out
or
this is war

said aggressively with no teeth showing =
he is annoying; we might be friends; enemies more days that not
or
I hate this guy, and if he looks at me one more time, I'm going to kill him
or
I love this guy so fucking much, it's making me crazy
or
he is my brother and a nobhead
or
this is war but one where I'm not going to put in my best effort because he isn't worth it

said cheerfully and with bared teeth =
I'm going to kill him gleefully
or
we're the best of friends
or
yay, because of him, we're going to war.

said cheerfully and with no teeth showing =
I love you so much
or
let's start a war for fun

Drazic demons *really* like going to war.

BASIC SENTENCE STRUCTURE IN WITCH DRAZIC:

verb-adjective > objectobject > subject
(ex: nom-ji taki, ij = <eat-quickly cake, he> = he eats the cake quickly)
for past tense, add "sek" to the start and end of the sentence/phrase
(ex: sek nom-maun taki, ij sek = <ate-slowly cake, he> = he slowly ate the cake)
for future tense, add "ba" to the start and end of the sentence/phrase
(ex: ba nom takimusal, ij ba = <will eat cake issing, he> = he will eat the cake's icing)
for questions, add "si" to the start and end of the sentence/phrase
(ex: si sek nom taki, ij sek si = <ate cake, he?> what do you mean he ate the cake?)

SUBJECT = MAGIC in the below examples

Valek ke zef <warm/intensify [moving/triggering/doing action] blood/life/love>
Pronounced: vay-lick kay zeef

boil the blood now

or

strengthen the love between us

Valek zef
Pronounced: vay-lick zeef

unclear whether verb is "to warm" or "to love"
(Magic will try anyway)

Valek ijzef
Pronounced: vay-lick ij-zeef

boil *his* (ij) blood (zef)
(Which is what Khalid should've said so he didn't get hit too)
if he'd just said *valek-ij* in Drazic (warm/intensify him), he could've
given his opponent an accidental power up. Yay Drazic.

Vicara, ke aloze <Win/victory/success/defeat another, [moving action] your home>
Pronounced: vee-care-ruh kay al-low-zeh

do what I want, I'll smuggle you back to your home

or

I succeeded in kidnapping you, now I will go to your home

or

kill him and the winner gets to go back to your home

Vicara vo, ke aloze alo
Pronounced: vee-care-ruh voe kay al-low-zeh al-low

I win, you go home.

Ke vovicara alo, ba ke aloze alo ba <[moving/doing action] my victory you, (future)
[moving/doing action] your home you]
Pronounced: kay voe-vee-care-ruh al-low, bah kay al-low-zeh al-low ba

You do what I want, you'll go back home.
(Varius should've said this to be more clear)

PLANE OF
MONSTERS

Those with the ability to phase do so by stepping through the Plane of Monsters, but given they move so quickly (a blimp of a second) and the world's one of constant darkness, very few people know this. All they know is that phasing is dangerous, and sometimes people just never arrive at their destination (because they get eaten by a monster – or knocked off their path by said monster and *then* eaten by it).

Witches, on the other hand, are well aware of the existence of this world as they use it for portalling, which is where they create two magical doorways in set places and then connect them. To step through the portals, they must also move a variable distance through the Plane of Monsters (distance dependant on a variety of factors, such as the size of the portal, the distance between, the power of the witch, etc), and they often get killed before they reach their exit as the light of our world draws the monsters to them like a ringing dinner bell.

After losing her older sister on one such trip through the portals, Coraima Vega dedicated her life to creating the first teleportation circle around sixty-nine thousand years ago. Using portalling and demon summoning as her groundwork, she invented a network of runic circles that allowed her to travel without having to go through that nightmarish world.

Despite teleportation magic being a lot harder to learn and control, the increased level of safety (do not confuse this with it being *safe*) has made portalling all but obsolete in the modern age.

In the Underground of Halzaja, there are "races" to see who can make it through the furthest portal or hold their arm, leg, dick, etc. inside a portal the longest. It's a very blood affair, very enjoyed by the [normally extremely drunk] participants (until they get hurt) and the betting spectators.

It is also used as a favoured execution method by gangs all throughout the Seven Planes as no one ever returns (the portals work one way). After Diega Ominara, an enforcer for the Sholov Gang on Blódyrió, got set up and screwed over by another member of the gang, his wife was forced through a portal. He went in after her, alongside his two brothers Kalik and Rorax, and he is the one the Shadow King made a deal with. They did not find his wife, but they did go back to Blódyrió and completely destroy the gang. Then they changed their last name to Shadow, moved to Earth, and created the Shadow Domain.

Those of the Shadow bloodline are the only ones who can enter this world and not get eaten by monsters. However, they can still fall off cliffs or walk into lava and die. They can also use this place as an etheric storage. They can put anything they want in it, but anything that radiates heat (such as a car's engine if it was just running) will be attacked. Maddox uses a cage to keep live people in. He also has a very strong freezer full of body parts that he uses in his shapeshifting magic. This allows him to change up in size during a fight, which isn't something shapeshifters can normally do as they need to collect the mass from somewhere else first.

Anything put into the world can only be pulled out by the person who placed it inside unless someone else goes in and grabs it. The location of it doesn't matter; sometimes monsters knock things around, but the magic of the caster will pull it out. If the item is in the same place, the portal opens above and sucks them out. If it has moved, the portal can open in any direction and rush towards them.

Shadows cannot use magic in this world, but other people (like Aleric with his phasing) can. This is not known due to how few people visit and return. There is a prophecy, however, that when a Shadow can call on their light in here, Raganarok will rise.

The Shadow family can also shift into a shadow. While in this form, they won't take any damage unless it's soul magic. However, they can't use any other magic in this form or travel up vertical surfaces that's more than three inches tall, so it is a bit limited. They do allow for faster travel though as they can streak at an Olympic sprinter's pace. They can't go through tall grass, across water, up a building, etc, etc.

Stronger Shadows can open up the portal strong enough to allow monsters to eat anything their shadows touch – both when they're in shadow form and when they are creating other shadows. Even stronger ones can open it up completely to allow the monsters out.

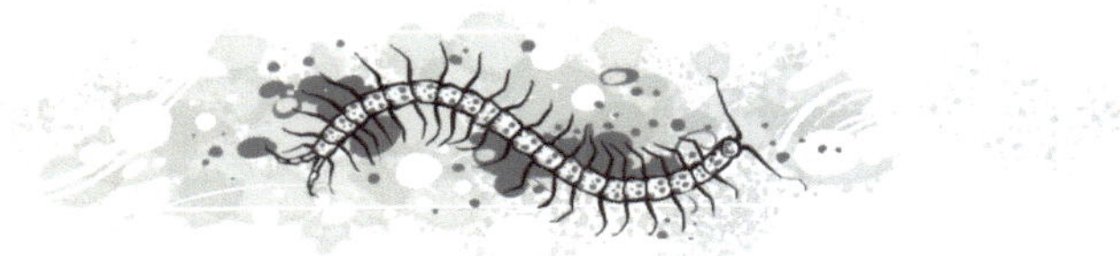

Believed to be a perpetual world of darkness, it wasn't until Sau Shadow spent some time here that it was discovered to have a very brief light cycle.

Arathnaetos

The monster Bonnie was an arathnae (plural: arathnaetos) – a truck-sized spider from leg to leg, making their body roughly the size of a husky. They have a black hairy body with a dark-purple pattern along their back. They live all throughout the Plane of Monsters, but they especially like the cliffsides and canyons as these places aren't as welcoming to the bigger monsters that will eat them. They actively hunt rodents, lizards, and snakes, but they'll eat anything that gets stuck in their web.

They build their webs every day, holding a liquid silk inside their bodies that then hardens into a solid once it hits the air. Their webs are often placed at choke points in canyons or just below narrow or crumbling paths on the cliffsides to catch those trying to squeeze through tight spaces or falling off ledges. Their webs range from the stereotypical shape of Earth spiders to large open cup-like cocoons that latch on to the side of a cliff and are strong enough to catch falling prey.

If they consume a human, that person's face will morph onto their abdomen, and their soul will be trapped on their body until the creature dies. The more humans they eat, the faster they get, and the longer they live. Legends claim there's a female arathnae out there somewhere who's been here since the dawn of time...

They don't stay on a single web all day. Instead, they make three or four of them and then migrate between the set. They don't need to walk across every thread to know if they have caught anything. They simply jump up and down on the centre mass, then pluck each of the threads attached to it. This causes vibrations of different frequencies to bounce forward and back, and they can then pinpoint what, if anything, is caught and where. Due to the strength of their webs, very few creatures manage to escape once they get caught. However, if any damage is done to the web, they can eat the surrounding section of it away, then repair it with more silk.

Female arathnaetos are over one hundred times heavier than the males. Most males don't bother to make webs as they spend the majority of their life roaming the world looking for a mate. This takes a lot of time and effort, especially in a world of perpetual darkness where they have to rely on their sense of smell and the luck of randomly finding wayward silk strands to follow.

Once they find a female arathnae, they can hang around her web, not touching it, for days or weeks – sometimes even months as they try to figure out a way/build up the courage to actually let her know they're there. Because if he does not approach her in the right conditions in the right way, she will eat him. Although she can tell from the vibrations he sends down her web just from walking on it that he's a male from her own species, that is not enough to allow him the right to enter her home.

So they wait until the female catches and eats a sizeable prey.

Then they rub their front legs together, sending out a vibration that is hopefully the one she wants. She's looking for one that's calm and soothing. Once she gives her first sign of approval, he steps onto her web and immediately starts dancing a serious of carefully choreographed steps that are sure to win her over. He stretches his two mid-back legs into the air, raises his ass, and shakes them all together. The bright colours of his back – a mottled purple and teal that they can see even through the gloom of the Plane of Monsters will tell her if he's healthy enough to choose as a mate. His dance will show her he has good enough genes to be coordinated and strong enough to pull off the intricate displays, as well as has the energy to finish it.

As he dances, he will inch his way closer to the female spider. At any point, for any reason, she can decide he isn't good enough and will eat him. As she is able to jump on him within fractions of a second, this is a very risky business, so his dance must be very precise.

If he manages to gain her approval enough to mate with her, it is a very quick affair. The longer he takes, the more energy she spends, the hungrier she gets. If he doesn't leave in time, she will grab him and inject venom into his brain, killing him quickly. So he crawls onto her head, turns her abdomen over with his front legs, and pushes his sperm inside her before scurrying the fuck off.

Once she is impregnated, she will lay one egg sac full of hundreds of babies. She will attach this sac onto her spinnerets, her silk-spinning organs located at the back of her abdomen, and carefully carry it around with her. If she loses this sac of eggs, she will try to find it. If she can't, she will pick up a rock or some other item and place it on her spinnerets to mimic what she has lost.

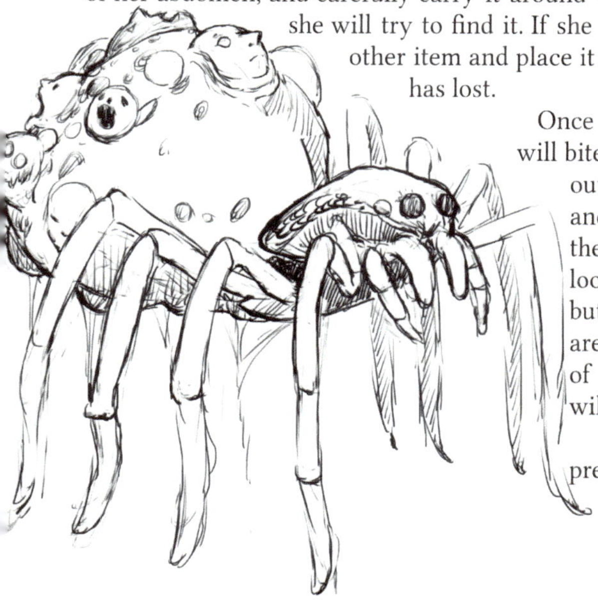

Once it's time for her babies to hatch, she will bite through the sac and help them come out. They will then crawl onto her back and stay there, hiding their legs beneath their body. The pattern on a baby's back looks like a screaming face for camo, but this will fade as they age. Once they are ready to leave, they'll spin a thread of silk to catch the wind, and then they will balloon away.

The hairs on their legs can be shot at predators as an irritant.

Echidnas

Named after Echidna, the Mother of Monsters herself, due to being her favourite children, these creatures are **not human** despite having a human form. They are true monsters that were created to fuck shit up in the Panhellenic Games after the gods said that none of the monsters she had previously made were that dangerous – including the dragons, as she hadn't instilled within them the urge to kill at any cost.

She'd done that to be *nice.*

So that the gods could have their fun rather than have their "little toys" enter an arena like a bunch of "old people" against a squad of nine-year-old pro gamers.

But now all bets were off.

For the next Game, she filled it only with six echidnas.

And they *slaughtered* the champions.

Some of the gods were pissed as fuck. Others were in awe. And then there was Zeus. He was so turned on, he gifted them with a **human form** so he could fuck them. He nearly died in that orgy, but he still claims it was one of the best nights in his life.

Echidnas are **extremely intelligent** monsters. They have keen depth perception, which allows them to calculate the precise location of their prey. Combined with their ability to phase short distances (about the size of a football field), they are easily able to ambush most things before they even know they're there. Even when fought head-on though, their phasing-striking combo makes quick work of their opponents.

Their two front legs are tough enough to pierce through a turtle's shell (dragon scales aren't that strong in this world as that would make it impossible for them to fly). They can shoot fine needle-like "hairs" from their back with enough force to pierce through the skin of most creatures. These hairs are also poisonous. If anything tries to sneak up under their legs –as they stand taller than giraffes– the echidna can curl up like a dying spider, wrapping their legs around the creature. On their underbelly is a series of claw-like retractable spikes. They can also twist their torso nearly all the way around, so they can cover every direction, and from a sac on their back, they can release a deadly toxin into the air like an octopus spraying ink as a last resort.

Despite their size, they are unnaturally quiet. They don't have a scent. They talk through chirps and clicks, but when on a hunt, they communicate telepathically through imageless "vibes" (like how a person with aphantasia "sees"), so telepaths can't read their minds either.

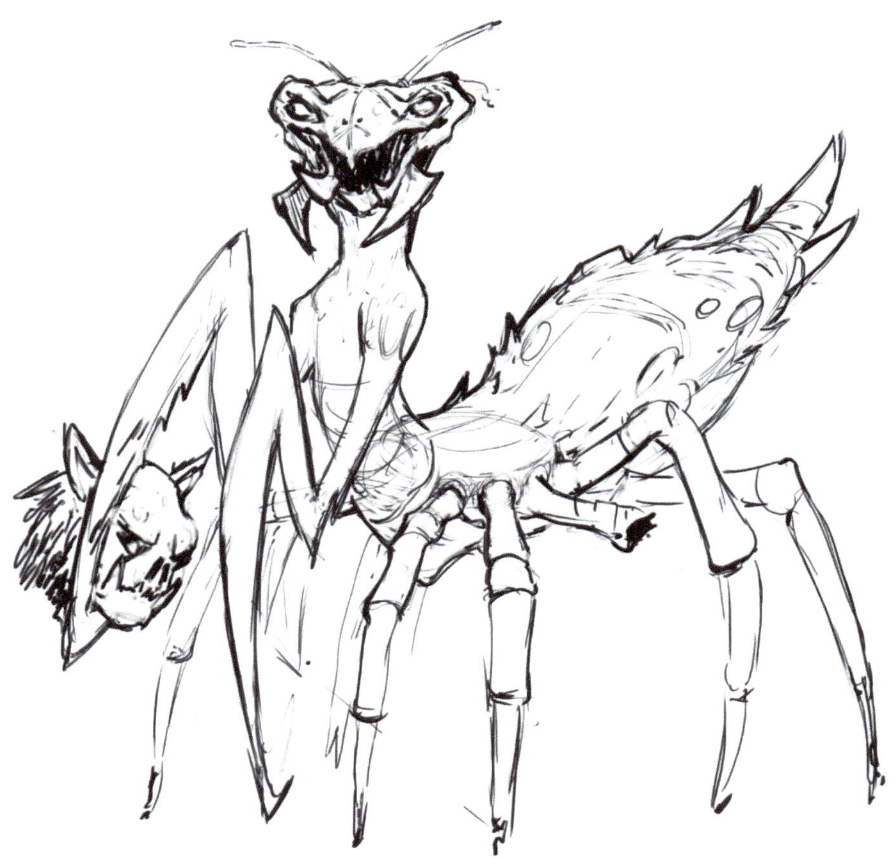

There are only a handful of echidnas left. The gods feared what would happen if they were quick breeders, so they only have an offspring every decade or so. Once the female gets big enough, it turns into a male. It is very rare to see one outside of the Plane of Monsters. There is one echidna in the Elv've'Nor, and she stays in her human form more time than not. She will never be reaccepted into her pack because of this.

Olivia, the monster that Sau met when she was in the Plane of Monsters and who now lives in their kitchen counter, was left behind by her pack for being a runt. When she started to die of old age (monsters do not heal like humans), Sau used her magic to bind her to the counter – a witch's kitchen being a special place. She needs to be fed blood (poured onto the surface of the counter) every so often, and the wood shifts as she moves. She can be brought out, but her life is now tied to the Shadow house. She cannot step outside of the grounds. Nor can she be outside the counter for long as her being bound to it is what keeps her alive.

Sau can often be heard singing and talking to her and seen running her hands over the wood in a loving pet. She keeps a keen eye on Olivia's mental health so she knows when it's time to let her baby go.

Monmons

The monster Sau called Molly, who was pulled out of her shadows when she met with Aleric and Antonio about the treaty, was a monmon. The females have a snake-like body and wings that flutter so quickly, they buzz like a bee's. They cannot use them for flight; instead their purpose is for communication – both for warning and for mating. The males, however, have much bigger wings that are used for flying. The reason for this difference is because females nest in a relatively small area, and the males fly over a much broader territory that contains multiple females. It's like the males having a harem but the females don't get along, so they all live separately.

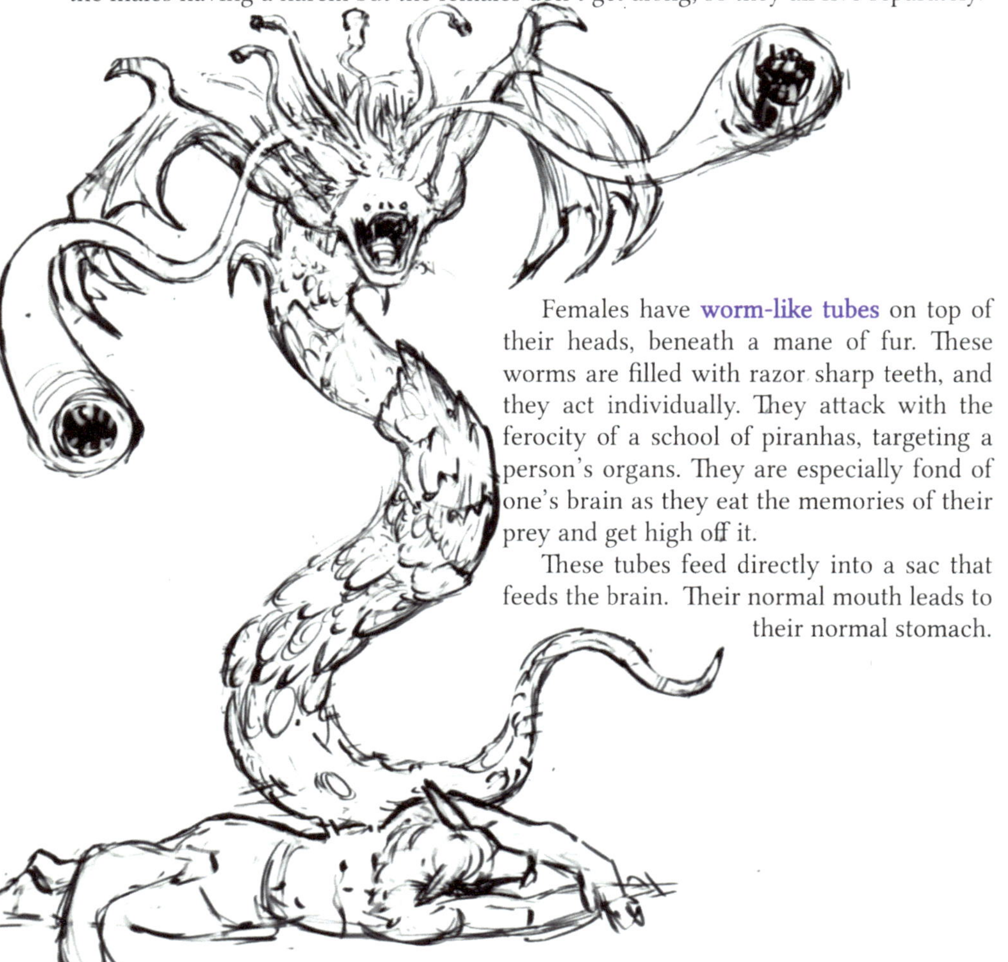

Females have worm-like tubes on top of their heads, beneath a mane of fur. These worms are filled with razor sharp teeth, and they act individually. They attack with the ferocity of a school of piranhas, targeting a person's organs. They are especially fond of one's brain as they eat the memories of their prey and get high off it.

These tubes feed directly into a sac that feeds the brain. Their normal mouth leads to their normal stomach.

Males have these same worm-like tubes on top of their heads and within their mouths. The ones in their mouths can be retracted, and they normally sit inside a special tube that runs parallel to their oesophagus.

They come out during **mating activities**, and they have special hooks to attach to the female's "worms". They then feed her regurgitated memories to show they are worthy of being her alpha. The bigger a male's harem, the more he has to prove himself.

Their **mating ritual** begins with the male catching the female's attention by swooping in on her from above. She rises up onto her tail and vibrates her wings in warning. Rogue males eat the females and their young, so they are always wary of them.

The male will continue to swoop closer and closer to her while pulling off a series of difficult manoeuvrers to prove his prowess in the air. He needs to get close enough to her to mate, but if she isn't impressed with his routine, she will try to kill him. If he is successful, they will then twist around on the ground together for a time while she checks his scent. If she approves of him, she will allow him to mate with her, which is when he holds her down with his hands and feed her his memories.

Monmons bond for life, but they **do not live together**. He will hop between his different harem members, so she will only see him the equivalent of a few months out of the year, rarely more than a week at a time, which is how she prefers it. Female monmons like to be left alone. She will lay eggs and then care for them until they're hatched. Once they're free, they're on their own.

The mated monmons will feed each other their memories throughout their life. This can cause fights if the female gets jealous of his other women. Sometimes, the female will even track down the other members in the harem and kill them and their children. If this happens, the male will then kill her as she isn't good for his harem.

The creature that attacks Micha in *Broken Souls* was Molly's child. Her name was Hoo-hoo, and she was a sweetie.

Stronabergs

A large dark-coloured cat with spots along its back, this beast can grow up to twenty feet long and weigh close to three thousand kilos. It lives in a pride of up to fifty members, all of which are female or juvenile. They do not have an alpha male, only bothering with the opposite sex when it's mating season. The males will hang around for two or three weeks before being chased off or killed.

The spots on their back are all
unique, just like a fingerprint is to a person. They range
from dark-brown to ruby-red. During **mating season**, the males' spots get brighter,
almost becoming reflective – proving they are strong enough to survive even with a
"beacon on their location". The two tendrils on their heads are semi-prehensile, and
they used to be slightly bioluminescent at the tips, acting as a lure to other creatures,
but as the cats evolved, they stopped relying on ambush techniques, so now the
tendrils are only used for mating dances. Their young are born with red quills on
their back that fall off as they age.

Jonathan, the stronaberg Sau pulled from her shadows in order to force Antonio
and Aleric to sign the first peace treaty of St. Augustine, was a lone male she found
during her time in the Plane of Monsters. He was only five feet long then, about the
size of a cheetah. However, they are much bulkier, having traded speed for strength.

Unfortunately, this is what allowed **Aleric** to kill Jonathan in the end. He phased,
then phased again in that blip of a second he was in the Plane of Monsters. He
assumed that if he kept phasing nonstop, he could still treat it as one hop, and end
up back on Earth – as long as he didn't stop for even a split of a second. He took a
pair of Sau's underwear with him and dropped it on the ground to lure her monsters
to him as he kept moving around the area. Her "children" know her scent, and they
always come running, so happy to see her.

Jonathan was the first to arrive.

After Aleric hacked his head off with a sword, he tried to phase to Earth, only to
find that his theory about 'it still being one hop' didn't fucking work. He survived
five days in the Plane of Monsters before Sau pulled out one of her babies, and he
phased through her portal with Jonathan's head without her even knowing.

THE SEVEN PLANES

Konistra

Every ten thousand years, the Panhellenic Games are held here. In addition to all the newly created candidates, one member of each previous winning race, called a champion, is plucked from the Seven Planes and tossed inside the games. If a champion is the last one standing, then no new race is created for the next ten-thousand (or more) years.

The terrain is designed to kill, housing rivers of poison, jungles filled with man-eating vines, quicksand that sets into stone, rain acidic enough to burn, fog that causes madness, etc, etc. And of course, there are monsters.

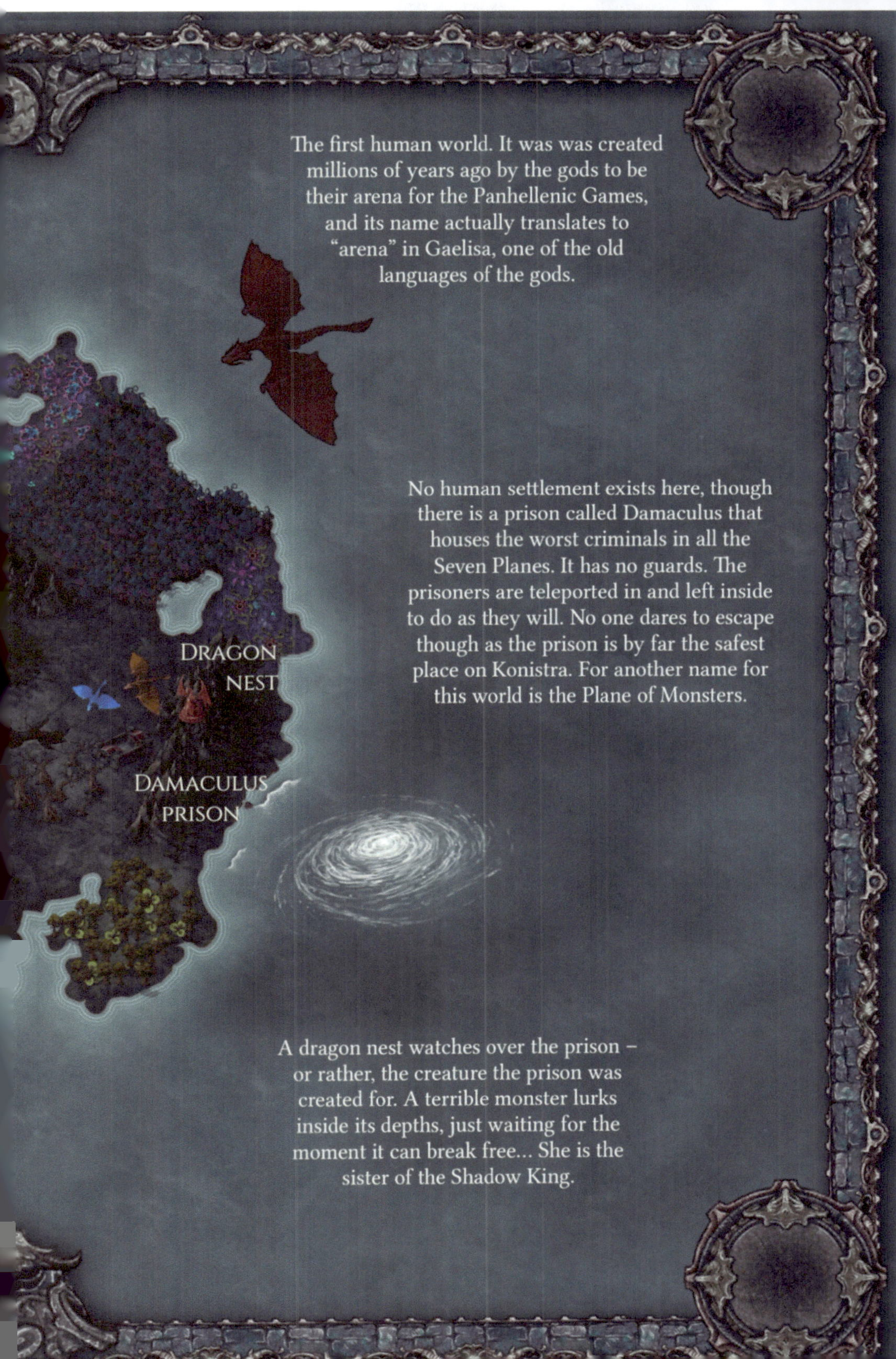

The first human world. It was was created millions of years ago by the gods to be their arena for the Panhellenic Games, and its name actually translates to "arena" in Gaelisa, one of the old languages of the gods.

No human settlement exists here, though there is a prison called Damaculus that houses the worst criminals in all the Seven Planes. It has no guards. The prisoners are teleported in and left inside to do as they will. No one dares to escape though as the prison is by far the safest place on Konistra. For another name for this world is the Plane of Monsters.

A dragon nest watches over the prison – or rather, the creature the prison was created for. A terrible monster lurks inside its depths, just waiting for the moment it can break free... She is the sister of the Shadow King.

Human towns are very primitive as they keep getting raided, razed, and raped by drazic demons. A town is often raided multiple times a day.

The angels live in the skies above. No map exists of their home as they do not allow outsiders in.

RUINS OF HEVANA

HELDRON

Raw resources are mined from Halzaja and taken to the other Seven Planes. It is a very lucrative business... if you survive.

Demonic entrances to the Underground
Human cities
Border of demon territories
Military towns that try to stop the demon raids

Halzaja

Sin

Sin is the only kingdom that trades with the humans rather than just stealing from them.

Ruins of Volskera

The outer islands are safer than the mainland as there aren't any demon kingdoms beneath them, but there's very little on them.

It is the age of piracy. Some ships are even captioned and crewed by drazics.

The sun is said never to rise or exist at all here, but in truth, it's just hidden by a perpetual curtain of clouds. Due to Artermis' magic, the moon still shines through.

Werewolves and vampires aren't allowed in any of the cities or towns an hour before or after moonrise in fear of the blood moon. Although the blood moon can occur during the sun's cycle, it's less likely to. However, not many wards can stand up to a pack of wolves under the Craving anyway.

The towns and cities are placed as far away from the woods as possible.

Blodyrio

Blood red moon bright and full –
Never venture past your door.
Blood red moon not yet full –
Fear the days of three or more.

The Blood Moon's cycle cannot be tracked, and it can appear at any time. It forces all 2 billion werewolves and vampires to fall under the Craving – regardless of whether they've had their ascension. Tens to hundreds of thousands of casualties occur by the time it's gone. Legends say this is when Artemis comes down to hunt.

Full moons are religiously tracked, and wards activated around towns and houses to keep out werewolves.

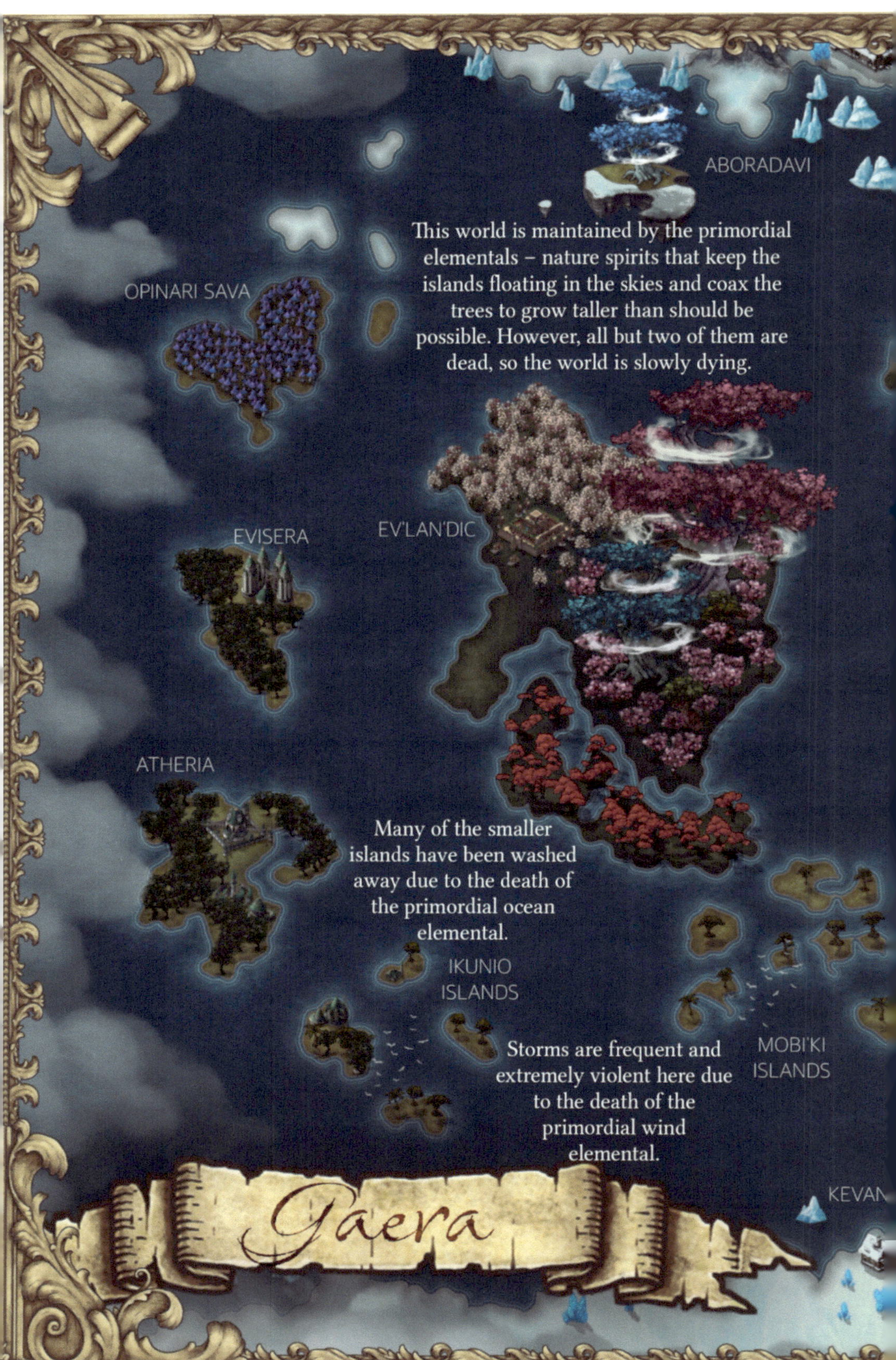

ABORADAVI
OPINARI SAVA
This world is maintained by the primordial elementals – nature spirits that keep the islands floating in the skies and coax the trees to grow taller than should be possible. However, all but two of them are dead, so the world is slowly dying.
EVISERA
EV'LAN'DIC
ATHERIA
Many of the smaller islands have been washed away due to the death of the primordial ocean elemental.
IKUNIO ISLANDS
Storms are frequent and extremely violent here due to the death of the primordial wind elemental.
MOBI'KI ISLANDS
KEVAN
Gaera

DESI FJORDS
VINSIO
ULAR
With the death of the primordial stone elemental, the mountains crumbled to half their size
LOST TEMPLES OF HONDU
This world is home to many monsters and creatures and care should be taken when outside of the cities.
BROWNSTON
Earthquakes occur regularly due to the death of the primordial earth elemental. The forests are dying, and the land is turning barren.
AIZELA
PISAMA ISLANDS
This is the only colony of dragons outside Konistra

Once home to the persapics – the umbrella
term for telepaths, telekinetics, and
astralists, Persic has now been abandoned
due to being destroyed during the Great
Extinction. No one visits it and comes
back.

Persic

All of the food comes from the north. Only vegetables are grown due to the lack of space for grazing. All meat comes from off-world.

There are more civilisations under the sea than there are on the surface.

ALAZUL

The crystals found at the equator are highly unstable. When they crack, they cause an explosion of ice crystals, tsunamis, and earthquakes.

The main cities are all on the southern pole. They have many of the best universities in the Seven Planes, and the biggest library is in their capital, Olivanu. Outside of Earth, this is the most technologically advanced world.

The supernatural world lurks in the shadows here. No government currently knows about their existence. However, with the growing numbers of WALL, that could change...

All werewolf communities are located somewhere close to either forests or mountains so they still have the freedom to hunt.

There are a few portals around Earth that are secretly active. The Shadow Domain controls the one in North America, and they use it to smuggle people – and now goods to and from Blódyrió.

EARTH

ENTRANCES TO UNDERWORLDS
PORTAL TO BLODYRIO
PORTAL TO GAERA
PORTAL TO ALAZUL
PORTAL TO HALZAJA

The lost city of Atlantis is rumoured to be the SCU's main base of operations. It's hidden somewhere under the sea, suspected in the Mediterranean, and is protected from being discovered due to a very powerful ward.

Europe is a hotspot for entrances to the underworlds due to the gods having vacationed here for a time. Hades was particularly fond of visiting Spain during the Moors time as they had wonderful libraries consisting of 600,000+ books.

The portal in Australia is deep in the outback, hidden under Uluru. It is one of the only open portals that isn't controlled by a gang.

The secret SCU prison is suspected to be somewhere in the waters off the coast of Antartica.

THE
AFTERLIFE

Outer Planes of Purgatory

A person is able to **choose** which of the three underworlds they will end up in. This is normally discussed with their loved ones if they wish to end up in the same place after death. However, first they have to make it there by going through the planes of Purgatory.

There are multiple planes of Purgatory, and they are divided into the outer planes and the inner planes. The **outer planes of Purgatory** are the ones closest to the world of the living. These are the ones you see when you're on the verge of death or when (or where) the veils between the worlds are thin. They don't look very different to your world, except for the whole "I can see reapers" thing.

Different reapers collect different souls, though only keres normally take those who've died brutal deaths on the path of vengeance because those souls are absolute dicks to collect. As keres are human, they're more capable of crossing into the world of the living to drag the suckers off it. Other reapers will take them if there isn't a keres around, but it's a much harder and more traumatic affair for all involved.

Sometimes, due to the **feud** between 'real reapers' (those made specially by the gods to collect souls) and 'keres' (those fucking egotistical humans who've come over here, thinking they can do a better job than we can), keres will deliberately leave a soul wandering around long enough that the other reapers have to collect them – as in they'll stand right fucking there, eating an apple and laughing as some poor reaper with a sassy mouth tells him to shut up and die.

Unlike real reapers, keres can actually die though due to only being human.

Not every soul is collected. If they are willing to walk on their own, they can go through the outer planes of Purgatory themselves.

The **inner planes of Purgatory** are further into the world of the dead, and to get to them, you have to travel through the outer planes. These are never connected to the world of the living unless something has gone seriously wrong. This is where reapers deposit the souls they collect so they can then pass through into the afterlife. Think of the outer planes like a shop, then the inner planes like check-out queues. Or the outer planes like a park, then the inner planes like a queue to play on the swings or slide.

There are three inner planes: Styx, which allows you to get into the Underworld; Tech Duinn, to get into the Otherworld; and Gjoll to get into Niflhel. Within these planes, you can still be pulled back to the world of the living, but it's very rare as a necromancer has to cross through the outer planes to get to you, then they have to find you amongst all the other souls – and your body has to still be in good shape.

Styx

A plane of various rivers and marshlands, Styx is named after its main river, the River Styx. This is the river souls must be ferried across by the ferryman Charon in his special boat as the water is extremely poisonous for souls to touch. If a human touches it, however, the part of them that touched it becomes invincible – their skin is all melted off and then replaced anew; this is not a pleasant experience. They will also be grabbed by the monsters within the river and dragged down to the murky depths to die, so someone needs to be holding on to them to pull them out. The place they are being held on to will not be invincible.

The river is hundreds of metres deep right from the edge of the bank, so you cannot walk into it either. Water from the river is extremely poisonous to drink and has only one cure – Charon's cum. However, he doesn't want to be sucked off by a dying, flesh-rotting human, so he's not really willing to help you out there. If a god drinks water from the River Styx, which is a punishment for them, they would be unable to move or speak for one year (a god year, which is different to a human's) and be ostracised for nine years after that.

To get across the river, you either have to pay Charon's fee or spend a hundred years wondering around Styx first. Once past the river, you'll reach the Gates to the Underworld, which are made of adamantine and guarded by Cerberus. Sometimes, he likes to chase souls and/or eat them, but they'll just come out in a few days, so all is fine. After walking through the Gates, you'll no longer be in Purgatory, and your soul cannot be collected by a necromancer. Now you are in the Underworld.

There are four other minor main rivers that make up the plane of Styx:

1. River Cocytus – a loud place as it carries sound from the Underworld. This is one of the two main hubs for the souls waiting to cross the River Styx as it allows them to communicate with anyone they know who is already inside.
2. River Acheron – the other main hub. However, this place is full of depression and misery as there's not much to do here to pass the time.
3. River Lethe – you can drink from this to forget all of your memories. Drink too much though and you'll forget you need to cross the River Styx so you can eventually be reborn. During the process of reincarnation, all souls have to bathe in the waters of this river.
4. River Phlegethon – water of molten fire that leads to Tartarus. This is one of the backdoors to the Underworld, and it has a family guarding it to stop any souls from escaping. Due to Tartarus being a prison housing the worst of the worst, these guardians are highly trained and always on edge. It is safer to go past Cerberus than it is them. As with all such guardians, they can grant the true death (ie: your soul will disappear, never to be reborn).

Tech Duinn

An island in the middle of a tumultuous sea, this is where the dead go to gather if they wish to enter the Gaelic Otherworld. It's ruled over by Donn, the Gaelic God of the Dead, and unlike the other two inner planes of Purgatory, it isn't a land of gloom and misery. It's a very fertile island filled with beautiful shorelines, nesting birds, wild roaming animals, and lush green grass and towering trees strong enough to withstand the winds of the ocean. The water is cold but not too cold to chill.

You will dive into Lake Burst, swim down to the bottom and collect a rock. When you breach the surface, you'll be reborn as an animal to spend your time here until it's time to pass into the Otherworld. The rock will hang around your neck, and it will read your soul to see where you'll then go. You are judged not by your actions in the world of the living but by your soul. It is a lot harder to not steal when you're hungry, to not join a gang when you've no other options, to fail to develop empathy when you're spoiled rotten. This plane looks past all those disadvantages and hardships, and it sees who you really are. That is not to say your actions while alive are dismissed entirely. The Donn judges you by character rather than circumstances.

Gjoll

Here, you will be judged not on your actions, like in Styx, nor on your soul, like in Tech Duinn, but rather simply on how you died. Despite Gjoll being the easiest way to "erase your sins", Hel is the gloomiest of the underworlds, and so it is rarely chosen.

To get into Niflhel, you simply have to cross a bridge. It has a roof but no walls, so it doesn't protect you from the cold, howling wind that's sharp enough to cut through the thickest jacket. Dark fog and mist cover the place, making it hard to see in front of you. If you fall off the edge of the bridge, you'll end up in the River Gjoll, which is full of knives (yay) and is cold enough to freeze your soul, turning you into an iceberg forever. While crossing the bridge, you will be faced with your darkest, most shameful, and most embarrassing deeds.

Once you get to the end of the bridge, you will then be told where to go.

Niflhel

Those who die in or because of battle will go to Valhalla. You will be forced to train every day as a warrior still as you will be used on the front lines of Ragnarok should it happen before you're reborn. But you'll also get amazing food, beds, and other comforts.

Those who sacrifice themselves for another will go to Freya's Hall. This is a field of meadows and wandering animals. It is a peaceful place, but you will be reborn quicker so as not to forget the hardships of life.

Those who drown or have their bodies dumped in the sea will go to Ran. This can be pretty traumatic for them as this place is at the bottom of the sea, but they do get turned into mermaids and krakmen, which helps them not be so afraid.

Hel is a dark, bleak world full of icy storms and mist. However, there is heating within the halls, as well as saunas, spas, and hot springs. As long as you're okay with spending your entire afterlife indoors, it's not too bad of a place. It just feels so utterly depressing, like the entire world is pressing down on you all the time.

Otherworld

After giving your rock to Donn, you can then pass into the Otherworld, which is ruled by Arawn. There are various islands, lands, boats, and other places to choose from or even move between should you wish.

All of the worlds are filled with festivals and wild nature, but there isn't any human civilization. No "luxuries" like running water, electricity, towns, etc. You will spend your entire afterlife as an animal, with no memory of who you were as a human.

You will not need to eat, but there is ample ale and "cat-nip" foods to indulge in if you wish. In some parts, it even rains ale. Life here is very good, but the reason it's not as popular as Hades' Underworld is because of the whole animal thing. For some reason that puts people off. Personally, I think that would be amazing.

Unless your soul is judged to be bad. Then you will be hunted down by the gods and slaughtered every day until your rebirth. Alternatively, you might be turned into a rock or stream or some other thing that isn't alive. However, if that happens, you will keep your mind. You will go crazy, but eventually, once you manage to meditate enough to reflect on who you are as a person, you'll be reborn. This "rewriting of one's soul" is another reason why the Otherworld isn't as popular. What you think is 'good', the gods might think is terrible... So the risk can seem quite high.

Hades' Underworld

After passing through the Gates of the Underworld, you will walk down the main road of the Asphodel Fields, which will cause you to lose all desire to go back to the world of the living. You will still retain your memories, but they will become ones of fondness rather than grief.

You will eventually reach a fork in the road, where you'll meet the Three Judges: Minos, Rhadamanthus (Rha for short), and Aeacus. They will then decide where you should go: back to the Asphodel Fields (though you'll be allowed off the main road this time), which is where the average soul goes; to Tartarus if you really were a bad little bunny – where you will suffer for eternity, never to be reborn; or to the Elysian Fields if you were a very good soul and should be given the gift of never having to suffer through hardships ever again.

Due to only the extremely good or bad getting split from the main pack, Hades' Underworld is much more like the world of the living than the other places.

The Underworld is ruled by Hades – a bookworm who only ever wants to be left in peace so he can finally get through his TBR (when he picked the place as his own, it was fucking empty, just the way he liked it. If he'd known souls were going to come and bother him all the fucking time, he would've picked the sea) – and Kore – a psycho maniac with a love for explosives, doggies, and her husband. Hades tried very hard to get her to leave when she first arrived though, going so far as to give her the Heimlich maneuver after she ate a pomegranate. Alas, she'd swallowed six seeds and was forced to visit every year; the rest, as they say, is history.

HOW TO ENTER THE UNDERWORLD WHILE ALIVE:

If a human wants to venture into the Underworld, you have to do the following:

1. **Build up your power.** An Earther or zilcher can only spend a minute or so in the Underworld without dying. A demigod can spend a couple months. If you want to bring someone back, it will take roughly three weeks to bribe your way through all the checkpoints.
2. **Find "gifts" for each of the people at the checkpoints.** You'll need something to bribe Charon, each head of Cerberus, and need a good story to get the Three Judges to let you past. You will also need actual gifts (not bribes) for Hades (who loves reading) and Persephone (who loves explosives, fire, and all around pranking fuckery)
3. **Make it through the Eleusinian Mysteries.** If you've killed someone, you'll first need to go through the Lesser Mysteries to cleanse your soul. These

take place in the spring, but the location of them changes after each one. You'll then need to go through the Greater Mysteries. These take place in the autumn, their location also changing with each new year. Here, you will learn how to separate your soul from your body without dying. It is similar to what you learn as a necromancer, so if you know necromancy already, you can skip steps 3 & 4.

4. **Catch a ride with a keres**. As these are the only human reapers, they are the only ones a non-dead person can catch a ride with. They only come to collect the souls of those who have brutally died on a path of vengeance, so you have to find someone who fits that and then either hang around until they die, hoping it's brutal, or you know... stabby stabby. Knifey. Knifey. Then temporarily tie your souls together in a binding circle so the keres can take you too. They're normally fine with this because a soul is a soul, and they'll get paid either way. On the off chance they don't, however, you'll need to try again.

5. **Bribe your way past Charon, Cerberus, and the Judges.** Charon will simply refuse to take you. Cerberus will tear you apart and eat you. The Judges will sentence you to Tartarus because violating the natural order of life and death is a serious offense.

6. **Fight the effects of the Asphodel Fields**. As you're alive instead of dead, the effects of the pollen will be significantly greater, and every time you inhale, you'll lose another memory. First the small ones that you barely remember anyway. Then the bigger ones, until you forget who you are and why you are here.

7. **Get an audience with Hades/Kores.** This can take a very long time – too long for you to survive often times than not. Hades is rarely seen, leaving the running of the place to his managers, and his wife... well... she might be better avoided. And at the end of the day, hopefully they like your gifts enough to let you go once your task is done.

www.ingramcontent.com/pod-product-compliance
Lightning Source LLC
Chambersburg PA
CBHW041732300726
48981CB00006B/326